DEAD ON DOUGHNUTS

SARAH JANE WELDON

Edited by
EDITING SERVICES INK

Isla Britannica Books

Dead on Doughnuts

BOOKS BY SARAH JANE WELDON FROM ISLA BRITANNICA BOOKS

Cozy Mystery Novels

Dead on Doughnuts

Extra Shots

Cupcaked Crime

Baa'd to the Bone

The Great British Stake Off

Ding Dong Merrily and Die

The Last Christmas

Let it Dough, Let it Dough, Let it Dough

A Grave Mistake

Murder in the Rigging

The Antiques Ghostshow

Your Mummy or Your Life

Pain in the Asp

Flight to the Death

Final Destination

Eternal Departure

Poisoned in Paradise

Peril in Paradise

Panic in Paradise

The Poison in the Soup

A Game of Cones

On Burrowed Time

What Would Agatha Do?

Fry Another Day

Short Stories

Morning has Broken

The Astronaut

Isla Britannica Books

First published by Isla Britannica Books in 2019
Text copyright © Sarah Jane Weldon 2019
Cover Design © by DLR Cover Designs
Editing by Editing Services Ink 2020
editingsvcsink.com

Proud to be a member of the Alliance of Independent Authors

A CIP catalogue record is available from the British Library

All correspondence to Isla Britannica Books
office@islabritannicabooks.com

This book follows **British English** spelling and usage.

DEDICATION

The book that you hold in your hands would not be possible without the love and support of my wonderful patrons and Kickstarter family. Thank you to each and every one of you from the bottom of my heart. Sarah xx

- Jean Curran - Barbara Fiedler - Tiffany Tyson
- Teresa Collins - Virginia Perkins Healy
- Mary Moon - Kathryn J. Rice - Carol Schmoker
- Aramanth Dawe - Belle Cheah - Mary C - Vikki
- Alwaysintrble - Teri Griffis - Nancy Pilot - Thyra
- Rokinrev and Winged Fox - Marcia Tyree - JJM93
- Nanciann Lamontagne - Virginia Perkins - Treasa
- Lynn Dawson - Dwayne Keller - Kristy C
- SwordFirey - Faith M. Nelsen - Anne Newman

- Kathleen from Idaho - Linda H - Tonia Williams
- Jolie Castilla - Gregory Tausch - Kathy Robertson
- Dianne Ascroft - Lucy-Jean - Sue Hampshire
- Madam Pince - Andrea Johnson - Polly Helms
- Valerie A. Bedell - D. Moreu - Rosie B - Katie
- Michelle Correll - Deana Potter - Bradley Walker
- S. Newell - Denise Cheng May Fong - Noelle
- Jerrie the filkferengi - Amelia Soon - Jenny Burdinie
- Fiona L. Woods - Beth Cheatham - K. Collier
- Thatraja - Chaim S. Weinberg - Lauren Ma
- GhostCat - Herbie - Katy Ratcliffe - Susan Schooler

ABOUT DEAD ON DOUGHNUTS

A COFFEE SHOP COZY MYSTERY ~ BOOK 1

A murdered chef. A poisoned pastry. Can a young barista deliver a killer their just desserts?

Maddy dreams of opening her own detective agency with her best friend. Fresh off her A-levels and looking to save up funds, she and her BFF take a gap-year job serving coffee to rich tourists at an Austrian ski resort. But when someone tampers with one of Maddy's sweet creations to snuff out a snooty pastry chef, the offending doughnut becomes a recipe for disaster...

With her dreams of becoming a PI in danger, Maddy has next to no time to preserve the cafe's reputation and clear her name. But as the suspect list rises and the trail of breadcrumbs grows stale,

Maddy's future rests on bringing the killer to justice.

Can Maddy close her very first case before she's cooked?

A Coffee Shop Cozy Mystery Series
Dead on Doughnuts (Book 1)
Extra Shots (Book 2)
Cupcaked Crime (Book 3)

AUTHOR'S NOTE:
This book follows **British English** spelling and usage.

There is a glossary of **Ski Resort Terms** at the end of the story

BEHIND THE SCENES

Patreon

Save money on my books by becoming a patron for $1 a month. Patrons receive all of my books for free BEFORE ANYONE ELSE. Plus, advance review copy Audible audiobooks, your name on the dedication page of future books, and my weekly Free Book Friday collection which includes all the latest free and hot new release cozy mysteries from a wide range of authors. Patrons have a dedicated community forum for getting to know other patrons and for chatting with me about new books, patron-only events, book signings, and life in general.

Patreon: patreon.com/SarahJaneWeldon

Watch Me Write in Real Time

I write live on YouTube most days, so if you want some company as you study or work then feel free to join me for a writing session live from my desk (or wherever else I might be). I also post unboxing videos of my new books, and plot and plan out new stories live with suggestions from viewers for things they would like to see in the next book.

YouTube: youtube.com/SarahJaneWeldon

Critique My New Stories

I share my daily work in progress on a website called Scribophile where you can read and comment on stories fresh from my desk each day.

Scribophile: scribophile.com/authors/sarah-jane-weldon

Buy Me a Coffee

If you've enjoyed my book or simply want to keep me powered up as I work on the next cozy mystery, you can treat me to a coffee on my Ko-Fi page.

Ko-Fi: ko-fi.com/sarahjaneweldon

New Book Alerts

Follow my Amazon author page for notifications of brand new books and upcoming pre-orders.

Amazon Author Page: amazon.com/Sarah-Jane-Weldon/e/B01KR2DYXA

Book Related Swag

You can grab t-shirts, hoodies, mugs, stickers, and lots more from my swag store. I'll be adding more book and character linked merch in time, so keep checking back or send in a suggestion for character specific swag.

Swag: teespring.com/en-GB/stores/sarah-jane-weldon

#cozymysteryday

Share your favourite cozy mystery books, movies, and more on the annual Cozy Mystery Day celebration day which takes place on 15th September (Agatha Christie's birthday). I created this special day in 2019 so that fans could share the cozy mystery love with the rest of the world. Simply follow and use the hashtag #cozymysteryday across social media, blogs, and you can always tag me on Instagram, Twitter, Facebook (@sarahrowssolo).

Val D' Isera Ski Resort

Snow Mountain Cafe

Emilio Silvestre - café *owner*
Sophia Saner - *pot washer*
Madeleine Cooke - *barista and sleuth*
Eloise Bates - *barista and sleuth*
Théo Messerli - *coffee shop regular*

Sébastien Paris Pâtisserie

Stefan Kress - *owner and Audrey's fiancé*
Audrey Flandin - *pastry chef*
Violetta Gruca - *kitchen porter*

Ski Resort Employees

Daan van Bree - *ski shop technician*
Nicklas Rehn - *ski instructor, Karl's brother*
Karl Rehn - *ski resort bartender, Nicklas's brother*

Sim MacDiar - *ski resort doctor*
Bastian Rainer - *ski resort police officer*
Bianco Bellissimo - *ski resort police officer*

SKI TOURISTS AND RESORT VISITORS
Camilla Vicini - *skier, mother to Francesca*
Francesca Vicini - *skier, daughter of Francesca*
Miryam Löfgren - *skier, Nik and Karl's cousin*
Margot Baillieu-Flandin - *Audrey's stepmother*
Félix Flandin - *Audrey's father*
Rose Landry - *Felix's secretary*

Part One

Oxford, England

Chapter 1

A-Level Results Day, St Winifred's School, Oxford, England: 16th August 2018

"I think I'm going to die," Eloise whimpered, clutching my arm for support as she ran her finger down the names on the school notice board.

I took a deep, nervous breath. "Me too. I can't look." I was desperate to find my name, but I was terrified of the outcome. What if I had failed my A-Levels? Or let us both down by not matching Eloise's grades? We had both studied so hard, and our future as private investigators depended on us getting into university. Our dream job could be over before it had even begun.

I felt a tense grip on my arm as Eloise let out a scream, shaking me out of my sudden onset of self-doubt. "Oh, my goodness! Maddy, I did it! I *actually* passed." She pulled me towards her, her finger now pointing furiously towards her name on the board. "Look there, you see it? Eloise Elizabeth Bates…Psychology A*, German A*, Chemistry A*, Business A*."

"Heavens to Betsy, Eloise!" I gasped, giving her a big hug. "I just knew you could do it, old chum." Eloise and I were huge geeks, and it was our life's mission to bring back all the brilliant expressions from the golden age of mystery fiction (even if we did seem a bit weird compared to our friends who used words like 'sick' instead of brilliant, and 'blood' when talking to classmates). It was our little thing, something that Eloise and I had started when we were ten years old and first came across the works of Agatha Christie. It was second nature to us now.

Eloise pulled out her phone, snapping a photo of her exam results - *just* to make sure her grades were real and she hadn't imagined them! Technically, we weren't allowed to take photos of the results board, but since the school wouldn't be able to give us detention or expel us for our behaviour, we figured there was no harm in breaking the rules just this once. Eloise was jumpy with anticipation, clearly relieved now she had the news she had waited all summer for. Which was more than could be said for me. My stomach was doing the tango, and my heart was worryingly starting to creep up my throat. Eloise patted my arm, sensing my anxiety. That was the great thing about having a best friend. There was no need for words, and years of boarding at school together meant that she knew exactly how to help me in my hour of need.

"Come on, Maddy. Let's find your results. I'm sure you'll do spiffily." Before I had a chance to respond, Eloise was hastily looking down the list trying to find my name. She had always been the braver of us, especially in kindergarten. Where I was timid and shy, Eloise came to life in any new situation. That's what made us a great team. Eloise focused on the bigger picture and I on the finer details. It had always been that way.

I inhaled deeply of the stale air of the hot corridor, pushing down my nerves as best I could. My hands were trembling badly. I hadn't been this nervous at the end of school drama production of 'Daisy Pulls It Off' - and I'd had the lead role in that. This was just ridiculous. Sure, I was naturally sensitive, but I wasn't usually a nervous sort. "I can't, Eloise. You do it. Pleeaasse! And if my results are bad, then promise you won't tell me. Just make them up." It felt childish to be such a drama queen. No one would die if I failed, but I knew that my results would shape mine and Eloise's future together, and I treasured my best friend more than anything else.

Eloise gave me a reassuring smile. But I averted my gaze, certain that I would puke or burst into tears, or both, at any moment. I imagined myself in one of those old black and white movies from the 1940s, a pitiful attempt to take my mind off my current predicament. Right about now, I, as the dashing lead actress, would faint on the spot, only for some charming young man to appear from nowhere and sweep me into his arms. I giggled at the randomness of my imagination, not entirely sure where the thought had come from. After all, our all-girls boarding school was, in fact, run by nuns. I leant against the corridor wall almost falling through the door of the toilet. The moment was hardly blockbuster movie material. Eloise tugged my arm, keenly aware that my attention and physical presence had wandered away from the exam results board.

It was a good job that Eloise was on the case, because had it been up to me, I might never have checked the results. She was well and truly focused. "Let me see, let me see. Carter, Chang, Chesney, **Cooke**. Madeleine Cooke. There you are, Maddy. OK, let's see what you've got. Oooh, Maddy look, look!"

Eloise had suddenly gone silent, her voice escaping her. It was not exactly helpful.

I still couldn't look. "Yes, yes? What does it say?" I spat out impatiently. "On second thoughts, don't tell me. I don't want to know *ever*."

But it was too late. Eloise had regained control of her vocal cords and out delightedly spilt my results as fast as her mouth could formulate the words. "Look, Maddy, look. You've passed! See here. Psychology A*, French A*, Business A*, Physical Education A*. By Jove, old fruit, 4 A stars. You really are a genius of the highest order."

I suddenly wished that I hadn't just told Eloise to lie about my grades. Now I didn't know whether to believe her or not. "Really?" I asked in disbelief. "You're not having me on?" It would be far worse than failing to now hear that I'd passed, only to discover I really had failed. Eloise was grinning something rotten, except I couldn't see her face because I had my eyes tight shut! But I could feel the strength of her glare and from the way she was violently shaking my arm as she chuckled, I knew she was speaking the truth. If I could only get my feet to move, I

5

might have taken a peek at the notice board for myself.

Eloise let go of my arm and snapped another photo on her phone before thrusting the screen in my face. I opened one eye cautiously. There was no denying it. Eloise could not have faked that photo. I shook my head in disbelief, grabbing the phone from her. Physically holding the picture in my hands gave me some sense of comfort, made things feel more tangible.

"Wait! Let me see that," I said, looking between the results on the phone and the results on the notice board. It really was the truth. Hours and hours of studying had paid off. "Eloise, I passed. I passed my A-Levels. We're going to be private investigators. It's real. I mean, it's happening. It's coming true. We did it!" Eloise was still nodding, clearly delighted that my reactions had at long last caught up with hers. Now we could celebrate together.

Eloise smiled as she said out loud what we were both thinking. "Won't be long until The Bates and Cooke Private Investigator's Agency opens its doors. Oxford's number one Detective Agency."

I pulled Eloise in for a BFF hug. "You know what this means, don't you?"

"I sure do," Eloise replied. "Teatime at Mrs Tiggywinkle's."

WE WERE JUST ABOUT to leave for Mrs B's tea shop in the city centre, when Mr Smith, the school's caretaker, appeared from nowhere, his face all twisted and wiry. "What's all this racket? Haven't you lot got better things to be doing than hanging around the school in the holidays?" Mr Smith knew full well that we were here to collect our exam results, but pretended as if we had randomly decided to break into an empty school.

"Sorry, sir," I replied. "We were just here to pick up our exam results." Mr Smith huffed. The other students had, of course, arrived before us to pick up their results, but Eloise and I had wanted to miss the drama of wailing teachers, parents, and students, so we opted to come as late as we could to miss all the fuss, much to Mr Smith's annoyance as we had now discovered. It really wasn't a big deal. Just an hour after everyone else, and still within the designated visiting time, and besides, Mr Smith was *supposed* to be at the school for the day, undertaking any required maintenance in preparation for the new term. There was no way that we were putting him out by arriving later than the rest of our classmates. He glanced at his phone for the umpteenth time and scowled as another message from his wife pinged loudly. We didn't need to be detectives to understand that she was waiting for him at home with a lovely chilled bottle of rosé and a barbecue that needed lighting. You had to make the most of the sunny days when you lived in Britain, and right now it was sweltering (as was Mr Smith's temper).

"Enjoy the rest of the summer, sir," Eloise said as we left Mr Smith to his sulking. It was odd to think that we would never have to see him again. That was it, our last time on the school premises. He would be the last staff member we would speak to and our last time as school students. How very odd. But at the same time, it was exhilarating as we began a new phase in our lives. There was suddenly so much to think about, a lot of unknowns, and for the first time, the freedom to make decisions completely by ourselves.

Once the initial excitement of our results died down, we somehow both drifted off into our own little private worlds, taking in the enormity of what the future might hold for us. We were so lost in private thought that it was a surprise to realise that we were now stood outside Mrs B's coffee shop called Mrs. Tiggywinkle's.

Luckily our feet knew the way, as we'd been visiting our favourite haunt ever since we were old enough to get permission to leave the school grounds. We frequented there for our group work, exam revision sessions, and in our roles as baristas, learning to make coffee and all kinds of tray bakes with Mrs B, who owned the coffee shop.

Chapter 2

Mrs. Tiggywinkle's Coffee Shop, Oxford,
England: 16th August 2018

No matter what day it was, or what the weather was like, the city of Oxford was busy. Wherever you turned your ear, you could hear a babbling conversation. A summer camp student sent to Oxford to learn English on an intensive course, or a tourist stopping abruptly in the middle of the pavement to exclaim how wonderful the yellow stone architecture was on some old college building. It was no wonder that the words of Oscar Wilde suddenly rang in my ear as I walked through the city's streets: 'Oxford still remains the most beautiful thing in England, and nowhere else are life and art so exquisitely blended, so perfectly made one.' Mr Wilde was not wrong, and it suddenly dawned on me that it would be hard to leave our 'home' now that the next stage of our life was about to begin. We'd dreamed of a gap year abroad after our exams for years, but now it was here, I found my tummy all aflutter with excitement and nervousness in equal measure. 'One step at a time, Maddy,' I reminded myself. Mind you, I could just be hungry; I'd turned down lunch because of my exam result nerves, and now my appetite had returned with a vengeance. One of Mrs B's pastries would certainly hit the spot.

I could tell from Eloise's expression that her thoughts were along the same line as mine. We had both been lost in our imaginations but were brought back to the present as we stopped on the pavement across from Mrs Tiggywinkle's and waited for the traffic lights to turn red. The coffee shop looked like something from a chocolate box painting. A large glass window, small awning, and resting against the wall were the black-framed bicycles with their little wicker baskets. After what seemed like an eternity, the traffic lights turned to red, and we rushed across the road as quickly as we could before the beeps finished their racy tune. It was going to be weird living in another country where even the day-to-day trivial things would be so different from the hustle and bustle of Oxford living.

Eloise sighed as her excitement of the exam results turned to reflection. "You know, I'll be sad to leave this place, Maddy."

She pushed open the glass door, the latch giving a little click before a small bell tinkled overhead. The coffee shop was heaving with exhausted tourists ready for refreshment and some time off their feet after pounding the pavements all morning. The coffee shop buzzed and echoed as visitors exchanged stories of museum visits and showed off their recent souvenir purchases. I giggled inwardly as I imagined them as conquerors or pirates now delighting in their treasure or spoils and I wondered whether Eloise and I would be like that when we visited another country. I couldn't imagine such things for too long. My brain was good, but it was not quite capable enough of maintaining a dream-like state whilst walking through the throng of coffee shop customers. The place was back-to-back with chairs and shopping bags, and it took a little longer than usual to make our way to the counter, where our boss Mrs B, was rushed off her feet. We were convinced that Mrs B had a sixth sense, because no matter how busy the place was, she always knew when we were there, even without averting her gaze from the plates she was piling high with scones, jam, and fresh clotted cream from a local dairy where her husband worked. We were barely through the door before she was calling across the coffee shop to us. We were sure going to miss her in our new jobs.

Mrs B handed a plate of rich, chocolaty éclairs to a quiet, nervous-looking Japanese man and smiled at him. "Arigatōgozaimashita" she offered, flashing him a wry smile. It took her a matter of seconds to free up her hands, suddenly raising them to her face in exclamation as she greeted us like an excited mother hen. "Oh girls!" She exclaimed. "I've been thinking about you all day. How did you get on? I bet you both did splendidly! I'm so proud of you, you've worked incredibly hard. Great things are waiting for you two, of that I'm certain." Mrs B spoke quickly. Frankly, I was surprised that she had found an opportunity to think about us for even a moment, given the long line of people currently waiting to order mouthwatering cakes and coffees from her. The place was manic, and the customers looked dumbfounded as Mrs B dropped what she was doing to focus all her attention on us. That was what I loved best about Mrs B, her spontaneity and zest for life; she was a bundle of energy and fun, quite the opposite of my parents, who were more 'corporate' - formal, composed, and minimal with the expression of emotion. My parents were typical stuffy suit-wearing lawyers, whereas Mrs B was warm and affectionate, wore loudly coloured clothing, and her reaction to our results made us both feel immensely special. After all, it was Mrs B's cakes that had got us through most of our revision sessions.

"We passed. We got all A grades," I said as Mrs B's face changed from worn-out coffee shop owner to proud cat that got the cream. Her eyes filled with tears, and as she wiped her hands on her apron, Eloise and I suddenly found ourselves in a full-on Mrs B bear hug, smothered with kisses and tears of joy. A bemused American lady pulled out her camera and took a photo of this rather 'quirky' Oxford moment. One to share with her friends at the bridge club when she got back home from her European trip. This image didn't exactly fit with what she had heard about Brits being 'stiff-upper-lipped' and 'emotionally stunted,' but she soaked up the scene all the same.

It was clear from the grip on Mrs B's hug that there was going to be a bit of a wait for coffee orders. She was in no rush to move on from this triumphant moment of happiness.

"That's my girls. Oooh, well done, you clever two." Mrs B finally and reluctantly released us from her grip and wiped a tear from her eye as she spoke in part to her confused customers. "Did you hear that? They passed. My favourite baristas passed their exams with flying colours."

"You mean, your *only* baristas," I teased with a smile. It hadn't occurred to me until now that Mrs B would have to find replacements for us until we returned from our gap year abroad. What if we didn't have our jobs to come back to? Mrs B wouldn't need four baristas, surely? I took a deep breath. Something to think about further down the line; I didn't need to worry about it right now. Eloise was always telling me to 'chill out' and to live 'in the moment,' and right at that moment there was a loud round of applause as a line of tourists in the queue spontaneously erupted into a congratulatory cheer.

As if suddenly remembering that there were actual customers in the coffee shop and that she was *supposed* to be running a business, Mrs B ushered us to a table and furnished us with two large marshmallow-topped hot chocolates and two China plates of assorted tray bakes. Out of habit, we found ourselves jumping up to lend a hand, but Mrs B would not hear of it no matter how busy the place was. "She will be alright without us, won't she?" I asked, tilting my head towards Mrs B who was now busy at the counter, rustling up a tuna melt panini for a man in a suit who looked like he'd had a tough day of deadlines. Mrs B smiled at the man, working her magic, his shoulders dropping the more he relaxed in her presence. He tried hard to move his clenched jaw, eventually managing a flicker of a smile. "That will sort you out," Mrs B winked at him as he handed over his change. "She'll be just fine," Eloise replied, and I knew that she was right. Eloise was always right when it came to people. It was one of her gifts.

Eloise put her hand inside the pocket of her denim shorts and pulled out a folded piece of paper. It was looking rather shabby now, but I knew instantly what it was. We had written it during one of our lessons at school when we were seven years old. We'd had a lecture on careers, and the teacher told us to write down a list of jobs we might like to do 'when we were grown-ups.' We wrote down a list of all the jobs that a private school would want to see, and then focused our attention on the second piece of paper, our actual list. Our secret list, our life plan. The one where we decided to become detectives with our very own agency based in Oxford. In a vibrant, people-filled city like this one, there were bound to be a lot of mysteries that needed solving. It made good business sense. Besides, there would be a surplus of doctors, lawyers, and accountants if our classmates were anything to go by!

"So then, Maddy. Now we've got phase one of our plan ticked off, it's time to focus on business." Eloise already had her game face on and had pulled out her notebook and a sparkly pen.

"How much have we got saved so far?" I asked as Eloise flicked through the pages and did some calculations on her phone.

Eloise and I had met at kindergarten when we were just three years old and had been in the same class at school for our whole lives right up until today. Now we had our exam results, we were done with school *forever* and it felt like the end of an era. Our whole lives had been building up to this point, and finally, it was real. Sure, we had made plans, and we both knew exactly how much we had saved up, but it was like we had to go over things again just to be certain that it was real, that we weren't just dreaming it.

We had planned our careers from an early age. We both loved solving problems and had decided that we would set up our own detective agency in the little premises next to Mrs Tiggywinkle's coffee shop. We were fortunate to have an allowance from our parents, but we decided to get jobs in the coffee shop so that we could learn about running a business, gain experience in studying people, and save up all the money we needed to buy our premises after university. Of course, we had never shared our plans with anyone else, because the grown-ups would never have taken us seriously. But we continued to work quietly behind the scenes.

We opted to become boarders at our private school, even though our families had homes close by. We knew that by boarding, we could invest our time in reading and watching murder mysteries and detective stories together and get more shifts at the coffee shop without our parents nagging us or asking too many questions. And now that we had both passed our exams, we would be able to have our gap year to earn some money and then come back to Oxford, ready to study at the university on our return. We had four years to get everything we needed to open our office, find ourselves some clients, and to build a reputation as private detectives. Eloise would study Forensic Science, and I would study Forensic Psychology.

Chapter 3

The Summer Party, Bleinheim Palace,
Oxfordshire: 18th August 2018

"These are delicious, Mrs B!" I exclaimed, my mouth full of the flaky pastry tartlet.

Mrs B had very kindly offered to provide the food for a summer party being hosted by Eloise's parents and my parents, supposedly in honour of our A-Level results and offer of a place at Oxford University the following year. But our results were really just an excuse for our parents to do some networking and brag about their recent successes or clients or how much money they had earned. They were lawyers in the same firm, and there was always a lot of competitive spirit amongst the partners and colleagues. It wasn't a world that

Eloise or myself much enjoyed or wanted to be a part of, but we knew we were fortunate and that we would never have met each other were it not for our parents choosing to send us to the private school.

"Maddy. Over there, twelve o'clock. What do you think he wants from her? Do you think she'll see through him?" Eloise whispered into my ear so no one could hear.

"I don't know. I think he has sussed out that she's getting a divorce and wants to take on her case so that he can get a large fee from her." I answered, eyeing up the lawyer and his potential client as they talked underneath the mulberry tree.

Our parents had been dragging us to these dull events since we were kids, but we had found our own way to keep ourselves entertained, and we made the most of the opportunity by using it to read people's thoughts, feelings, and motives. Then, at the end of the party, when our parents were dissecting the information they had got out of each conversation, Eloise and I would see who got the most things right and who scored the most points in our little game. It was all perfectly innocent, but it made the parties and networking events a little more bearable.

"Ah, there you are, Maddy. I've got someone

I'd like you to meet." My mother looked especially beautiful in her summer dress, and many eyes were upon her as she breezed across the patio of the mansion house towards the corner where Eloise and I were hiding.

"This is Audrey Flandin, daughter of Félix Flandin. You know the man, Daddy's partner in the Paris office. Audrey, this is my daughter Madeleine. She's a keen baker like you; she makes the best cakes. Well, girls, I'll leave you to it. I'm sure you have a lot to talk about." My mother turned on the spot with elegance and wafted off, casting smiles and greetings at the guests as she went.

The girl Audrey looked quite sour as she surveyed Eloise and me from head to toe as if we were covered in filth. "So, I hear that you bake, do you? Where exactly did you train?" Audrey raised a perfectly painted thin eyebrow at me as she stared at my face. She was a few years older than me, possibly 20 or 21, and it seemed that my mother's reference to me as a baker had caused her great personal offence.

"Oh, Maddy makes the *best* cakes in the world. They really are good. You should come and try them one day. We both work with Mrs B, who made the food for the party in her coffee shop, *Mrs Tiggywinkle's*." Eloise pretended not to notice Audrey's disgust.

"How many stars does it have? Is it a Michelin?" Audrey looked at me seriously, and I suddenly felt quite uncomfortable. She was certainly not an easy person to warm to.

I was determined to keep the conversation light. After all, I had done nothing wrong, and there was no need for her spiteful attitude. "Umm, no. I've not got any formal training. Mrs B taught me, and it's the best coffee shop in all of Oxford. I don't think it needs any Michelin stars. Customer approval is perfectly sufficient. That might even put people off coming if they thought it was all la-de-dah and not a cosy coffee shop with mouthwatering cakes."

Audrey looked set on steering the conversation back to her own accolades, as if making a point that we were not to be considered in her league in any shape or form. "And what do you study? Or are you still at school?"

"We just received our A-Level exam results a few days ago, so we're going to have some fun adventures on our gap year now, and then in September next year we'll start our degrees at Oxford University." I felt that I was as polite as I could be, and I wasn't going to be drawn into any competition with her, nor did I have anything to prove to an irritating person like her.

But Eloise was not letting Audrey off so lightly and decided to probe further, knowing that the girl would not be satisfied until she had told us whatever it was that she felt we needed to know about her. "And what about yourself? Do you live in Paris like your father?"

"Actually, I'm at St Joseph's Culinary School in Paris. Well, I've just finished. I'm a fully trained pastry chef, and Father is going to buy me a business so I can have my own shop."

Eloise looked gruff. Like me, I could sense that she was struggling to work out this strange girl, but she was genuinely impressed by the idea of someone so young owning their own business, and it would be useful for us to get some insight for when we finally set up our detective agency. "Wow, you really are passionate about business; that's incredible. How very exciting. I bet you can't wait to get stuck in with designing your own shop and seeing all those customers enjoying your pastries."

Audrey seemed bored with us already. The words came out of her mouth, but her eyes glazed over, suggesting that she was scanning the party for someone more interesting to speak to. "Not really. To be honest, I'm not even sure if I can be bothered with having my own place, but it keeps my father happy and stops him interfering. Very soon I won't need to work at all, because I come into my own money when I reach 21, so I'll probably just retire and sit by the pool all day."

It was the wrong moment for Eloise to take a sip of fizzy champagne, and it almost resulted in Audrey getting a face full of spray as Eloise did her best to control an outburst of laughter. "Aren't you a bit young to retire? I mean, don't you want to do something with your life first? So many opportunities open to you —I don't know, like travel, or volunteer, or well, do anything? Won't you be bored sitting by the pool all day?"

"Bored? Gosh, no. I'd have my friends over like we do every summer at our chateau in St Tropez. There are too many parties to get bored. Like *proper* parties." Audrey looked around her to insinuate that this was not a party but a mere amateur event. I was already struggling to find things to like about this arrogant girl. I would kill my mother later for dumping her on us like that. Audrey was simply vile.

"Well, Eloise and I can't wait to start our adventure. We've got jobs as baristas at the Snow Mountain Café, in the Val D'Isera ski resort, in Austria. We applied ages ago without our parents knowing. Of course, we've told them now that we've got our exam results, but we didn't want the grief of having to convince them about us taking a gap year before university. We'll be working at Mrs B's coffee shop for the rest of the summer before we leave in November, ready for the ski season."

I was keen to inject a bit of energy into the conversation because I felt myself getting annoyed and wanting to bop Audrey on the nose, and I sensed that Eloise wasn't far behind me in the punching stakes.

It was Audrey's turn to laugh and sneer. "Val D'Isera. Pah! You wouldn't catch me there in a million years. Father says it is simply the worst resort in the world. It's full of, you know, common people and nouveau rich. Why on earth would you want to go there? Couldn't you get a job in a better class of resort? And to work in a coffee shop of all places; how dull!"

Eloise was gritting her teeth. "Actually, I'm looking forward to it. We'll be able to go skiing and snowboarding for free whenever we want, and it'll be great to be in the coffee shop meeting all the resort staff and guests. We'll be at the hub of the community, earning our own money and saving for our future."

Thankfully, Father decided to make a toast at that moment, and as he raised his glass and said a few words to the crowd about how clever we were in passing our exams, Eloise and I took a step closer to him and smiled, as much to get away from Audrey as anything else. The girl was exhausting, and we hoped to God we would never see her again.

Part Two

Paris, France

Chapter 4

Sophia Saner, St Joseph's Culinary School,
Paris, France: 29th August 2018

Sophia slipped her thin arm into the silky sleeve of her graduation robe and pulled the cloak up and over her shoulders. She couldn't believe that this day had finally come after all those hours of slaving away in the coffee shop and taking on work as a cleaner just to make ends meet. Finding the tuition fees alone had been a mammoth task that seemed impossible, but somehow, she had pulled it off. She placed the graduation board on her head and looked at herself in the mirror. She was 20 years old, but already her face was wrinkled, and she could see large black bags under her eyes.

"Don't worry, Sophia," she said to herself as she opened her eyes as wide as she could to try and wake herself up. "Life is about to change; the hardest part is over." Sophia turned to the side. She was pleased with how well the gown fit her, and she was ready for the next stage of life to begin.

It should have been a difficult day for Sophia, surrounded by her classmates as they were fussed over by doting parents, but somehow, she just accepted things, and it made her prouder than ever to know that her success was one hundred per cent her own. She did not have parents to fund her or to bail her out so she could buy the best culinary knives or pastry rollers. She had earnt her success through her own blood, sweat, and tears.

A girl approached her after the ceremony. Sophia recognised her immediately. It was Audrey Flandin, daughter of billionaire Félix Flandin, heiress to a fortune. Sophia didn't know her that well, but she knew that she didn't much care for the girl. She was always gloating, and everything seemed to be handed to her on a plate. Rumour had it that Audrey had paid the other students to do her kitchen prep work and assignments and had barely lifted a finger herself. She knew Sophia's name, of course, but she rarely used it, and only really spoke to Sophia when she wanted something or wanted to big herself up in front of the others.

"Oh, hello. Sophia, isn't it? I'm Audrey."

"Yes, I know perfectly well who you are. You're the girl who likes to borrow people's pastry kit and then fails to return it." Sophia was usually polite to Audrey, but she didn't feel the need to tolerate her any longer.

"Haha. You have a funny sense of humour. I'm sure you could buy some new kit if I didn't return it. Why didn't you simply order a replacement, as any other chef would? Honestly, some people. So fussy and possessive about objects. So materialistic." Audrey was unsympathetic to all the extra shifts that Sophia had put in just to buy the basic equipment she needed for the course. Or how those extra shifts had impacted on her study time and amount of sleep she was able to snatch each night.

"Look what Father just bought me. Isn't it divine? Real diamonds and everything. Of course, it's just costume jewellery; I have other watches for special occasions. This one is for everyday wear." Audrey lifted her wrist to Sophia, the diamonds catching the light as she waved her arm under Sophia's nose.

Sophia was sulky. "I suppose, if you like that sort of thing."

Audrey flicked her wrist away, not wanting Sophia to get her filthy hands on it. She clearly didn't appreciate a quality watch when she saw one, but then that was no surprise, given her parentage. Of course, Sophia's parents had died long ago. "Did I tell you I'm off to St Tropez for the rest of the holidays? I am so looking forward to a rest after all the stress of the course. How about you; do you have any plans?"

Sophia felt smug for once. It wasn't often she had news worth celebrating, but things were on the up for her, and she couldn't wait for Audrey to find out about her new job.

"Well, I'll be starting as a pastry chef, of course. I've got a position with a Michelin star chef at a highly regarded restaurant in Austria. I start at the end of November before the ski resort guests arrive."

Audrey was irritated. She had no great desire to be a pastry chef, but she knew how annoyed her father would be to discover that this low-class girl had got a better job than his daughter. Audrey didn't like to be second best to anyone, and right now she hadn't applied for any jobs. "A pastry chef? I'm sure you must be mistaken. Surely you don't have enough experience to go straight in at that level?"

Sophia felt triumphant as she produced a crumpled piece of paper from her trouser pocket. It was a job offer, and it was a golden opportunity to rub Audrey's face in her own glory after years of being bullied and made to feel worthless.

"Oh, I'm absolutely certain. You see: Sophia Saner, Head Pastry Chef for the Sébastien Paris Pâtisserie at the Val D'Isera ski resort in Austria. Doesn't get much better than that, does it?"

"Haha. Val D'Isera; you do know that no one who is anyone of importance goes there anymore, right? I'm surprised there is a Michelin star restaurant there at all, to be honest. It won't keep its stars for long if you're their head baker, let's be fair." Audrey sniggered, but she was quite obviously upset by the news.

Audrey was keen to leave this conversation, and right now, any conversation would do. She spotted a tutor she didn't much like, but it was the only opportunity she could muster up for a hasty exit.

"Oh, Miss DuValle, I wanted to ask you about one of your recipes."

Audrey walked over to Miss DuValle, leaving Sophia feeling like she had won a battle for once.

Yes, things were on the up for Sophia Saner. Just a couple more months of washing pots in the cafe, and then she would be in Austria, employed in her dream job.

Chapter 5

Audrey Flandin's Penthouse Apartment, Paris, France: 29th August 2018

udrey typed the words into the search bar on her computer:

Stefan Kress, head chef, Sébastien Paris Pâtisserie, Val D'Isera

IMMEDIATELY, the computer sprang into action as pages and pages of related search results lined up below the search bar. This Stefan truly was the king of pastry chefs, and his restaurant had won many awards. It seemed to be going places, and fast.

"Why on earth would they want some skinny girl like Sophia on their payroll? That makes no sense at all," Audrey spoke out to herself, tapping her painted nails on the desk in front of her. "Sophia Saner, Head Pastry Chef indeed. Well, we'll soon see about that."

Audrey picked up her iPhone. "Call Father."

The phone gave a little beep, and an automated assistant replied to her command, "Calling Father for you now." A few seconds passed as the phone dialled the number and her father fumbled around for his phone.

"Hi, Daddy, it's me. Listen, I've something important to tell you. I've had a long hard think, and I've decided that I don't want to go to St Tropez after all. I want to get a job at the Sébastien Paris Pâtisserie in Austria instead."

Audrey's father, Félix, was matter-of-fact in his reply, well used to the sudden whims of his daughter. "OK, darling, I'll have Rose sort that for you. Anything else?"

"No, Daddy, that's everything." Audrey hung up the phone, knowing full well that her father's secretary, Rose Landry, would have her a job as a pastry chef at this Stefan's restaurant by the morning. She just needed to find an apartment to live in close to the restaurant, and her father could have one of his planes drop her off. She would leave as soon as possible; she would need to get a head start if she wanted to get Sophia's job.

morning. She just needed to find an apartment to live in close to the restaurant, and her father could have one of his planes drop her off. She would leave as soon as possible. She would need to get a head start if she wanted to get Sophia's job.

Chapter 6

Sébastien Paris Pâtisserie, Val D'Isera, Austria:
20th November 2018

"Well, what do you think?" Audrey removed the silver teaspoon from Stefan's mouth and ruffled her hand through his hair. She had been dating the owner of the Sébastien Paris Pâtisserie since just a few days after arriving at the ski resort, and the couple had recently got engaged. It was nearly the ski season.

"It's OK, but I think it needs a little more vanilla."

Stefan ruminated for a few more moments as

he tried Audrey's latest concoction. She was OK at baking, but she didn't quite have the wow factor, and he didn't want the restaurant's reputation to suffer as a result. Of course, he couldn't tell Audrey that. Not if he wanted to keep dating her. So he did what he could to be firm but fair, encouraging but not untruthful. He was already on his second wife and had recently been dating another young lady, who he had been sure was the one, but then Audrey had come along, and he had been swept away by her strong will. She was a tough lady to say no to, and her father was even tougher. If he could keep her father on his side, then it would do no end of good for the restaurant, and he wanted her father to bring in new clients.

"OK, try this one. I added a little something special to the pastry to make it a bit lighter in the mouth." Audrey pressed the spoon edge downwards and into the flaky pastry, scooping it up, ready for Stefan's taste buds. But the taste test would have to wait. His phone was ringing.

"Sorry, sweetheart, business call. We'll continue this later." Stefan kissed Audrey on the cheek and ran off, phone to his ear.

Audrey gathered up the collection of side plates and removed them to the kitchen. She looked red and angry. How dare he walk out on her like that. She should be his sole interest always. But it was work, work, work with him. Only ever interested in his precious stars for the restaurant.

"How did it go, Audrey? Did he like them?" Violetta enquired as she loaded up the dishwasher in the restaurant kitchen.

"What? Of course not, how could he? I tell you now if I can't get him to like any of these cakes before ski season starts, then I'll be after your blood." Audrey was fuming.

Violetta quivered with fear. It wasn't her fault that Stefan hadn't been gushing over her cakes. After all, she was just the new girl, and she certainly wasn't a pastry chef. Stefan had employed her to work as the kitchen porter for a season. Never in a million years had she expected that she would be doing all of Audrey's work as well as her own. The plan was to spend her free time outside of work out on the piste snowboarding, but instead, she was being blackmailed by Audrey and given twice the workload and three times the bad attitude. It was so unfair.

Audrey shouted at her. "Get this lot cleared up." Violetta bit her lip and did as she was told.

She'd only been in her new job a matter of days, and already she wanted to quit. Stefan seemed nice enough, but Audrey had him wrapped around her little finger, and whatever Audrey said to him impacted on all the staff at the restaurant.

Chapter 7

Flight SA129 to Austria: 28th November 2018

"Oh, fiddlesticks! I was hoping to have the window seat," I exclaimed as I looked down at my plane ticket. "At least one of us has it. I hate being in the outer seat."

Eloise shuffled towards the window seat; there wasn't a lot of room at all. "Well, at least it's only a short flight, and we are seated together. It could be worse."

Eloise was right, and as I glanced around at the other passengers, I felt quite lucky with our flight arrangement.

"On the plus side," I said, "I might get to sit next to a handsome young man for the whole flight." We both giggled.

"I bet you get some horrible or smelly person next to you now," Eloise smirked as a girl of about 20 years old approached our row and double-checked the seat number on her ticket. She smiled nervously and stowed her bag in the overhead locker before taking her seat, buckling up the belt, and making herself comfortable.

I was never good with social situations, but I thought I should at least try to break the ice. Otherwise, the flight would feel long and weird. "Hello, I'm Madeleine, Maddy for short, and this is my best friend, Eloise."

"Oh, pleased to meet you. I'm Sophia." Sophia reached out a hand to shake ours; she was very polite and quietly spoken. I was relieved that she seemed to be friendly.

"Oooh, are you French?" Eloise piped up.

"Yes, I am. But my flight connected in London and I had to change planes. So now I've been to two countries already in one day. And by the time we get to Austria, I'll have been to three countries in the space of a few hours." Sophia was just as excited about flying as we were, it turned out, and we chatted for the entire journey.

"So, you're going to be working in Val D'Isera ski resort!" Sophia cried, clapping her hands together. "I can't believe it. What are the chances? That's where I'm heading too. I've got a job at a restaurant for the winter season. Longer if all goes well."

It certainly was a coincidence, and Sophia seemed kind and warm, so we were delighted to have made at least one new friend already. Eloise was keen to talk more, to see what else we might have in common.

"Ooh, we've got jobs as baristas at a coffee shop there. It's called the Snow Mountain Cafe. You'll have to pop in and have a coffee and cake … on us. See what you think of the place."

"I'm not sure how happy the new boss will be about you giving away his coffee for free, Eloise," I laughed, but I knew that I would have offered the same to our new friend.

"Well, I don't think I could accept a free drink from you, but I'll certainly come and see you. It will be nice to have people to visit, for sure." Sophia's face lit up as she smiled.

We were chatting so much that the flight passed quickly, and by the time we arrived in Austria, we had already made plans to share a taxi to the resort, since it had turned out that we would be sharing the same staff chalet, and to visit the glacier once we all had a day off. We were going to be the best of friends.

Part Three

Val D'Isera, Austria

Chapter 8

Ski Chalet, Val D'Isera resort, Austria: 29th November 2018

"I don't know about you, but I was too excited to sleep, so I decided to get up early and make crêpes for everyone. I hope you like them; otherwise, I'm going to get very fat eating them all myself." Sophia pointed towards a very large pile of perfect French crêpes on the chalet's kitchen counter. It was a tight space to cook in, all wood-panelled. To be honest, we were amazed that Sophia could magic up anything in what was effectively a broom cupboard with a larder that seemed bare.

"These smell divine," I said.

"To die for," Eloise added.

"I just hope that my boss likes my cooking. I'm so nervous, but my head is already full of pastry ideas for the restaurant. I don't technically need to go in until this evening, but I'm going to swing by anyway, just to get my bearings, make a good impression, you know." Sophia was far more awake than the rest of us, and her arms were waving around manically as she spoke.

"I think we should probably get going, Maddy. We don't want to be late on our first day; otherwise, we won't have jobs to go to." Eloise grabbed a handful of crêpes for the short walk to the Snow Mountain Cafe. I wanted to gobble down more too, but I had butterflies in my tummy and thought it wouldn't look too good if I was sick on the boss for my first day.

"OK, see you later, Sophia; thanks for breakfast. Hope you have an amazing day. We'll catch up later," I said as I followed Eloise out the chalet door.

It was lovely to step out into the fresh layer of new snow, especially after living through a rainy and grey November at home in Oxford. It was our first day in Austria, and though the air was cool, it wasn't damp like England, and the sky was clear blue and full of sunshine. The air smelled so pure, free from the pollution of traffic and grime up here in the mountain air.

Eloise was still chomping away on crêpes, and I was busy concentrating on my footsteps as my feet sank into the deep snow. I still couldn't quite believe that we were here.

"Sophia seems nice," I said. Eloise nodded. "I hope our new boss is just as lovely. It's going to be weird working for someone new after working with Mrs B." Eloise nodded again, her mouth still full of food.

We turned a corner, and there it was, the Snow Mountain Cafe, with its glass windows and door. It seemed a lot bigger and more modern than Mrs Tiggywinkle's at home in Oxford, and it was certainly a lot less busy. It seemed new and shiny, more modern, like those pictures of contemporary New York loft apartments. It had an air about it that drew you in, warm and welcoming, especially when compared to the snowy street outside. We kicked the snow off our boots and pushed the glass door open, instantly greeted by a rush of warm air and the smell of sweet hot chocolate and baking.

I followed Eloise to the counter, only too glad that my best friend was far less of a coward than me. Eloise spoke to the man first, whilst I observed and nodded where I needed to. The butterflies were suddenly returning to my tummy.

"Hello, I'm Eloise, and this is Madeleine; we're your new baristas." A tall thin man with a tight V-neck shirt and necklace threw his olive-coloured bare arms in the air and rushed around the counter to greet us, taking us quite by surprise. "Ahhh, welcome, welcome. I'm so happy to meet you both." He air-kissed us three times on alternate cheeks in a rather dramatic way, his arms clasping ours in a warm embrace. "Welcome to the Snow Mountain Cafe."

I finally found my voice, probably from the shock of such an over-the-top welcome. "Thank you so much for giving us the jobs, Mr Silvestre."

"Oh, no, no, no, no." He replied, waving a long finger at us. "Please, call me Emilio."

"Emilio, OK," I said, glancing around the coffee shop. It was empty apart from a man in his thirties, who was sat by the window, doing a crossword from the resort's newspaper. Emilio enticed us over to the customer, one hand on each of our backs, pushing us gently forward.

"Girls, I want you to meet my best customer Théo Messerli." Emilio pushed us forwards a little more so that Théo could see us properly.

"I think you mean your *only* customer," Théo replied with a teasing smile on his face as he winked at Emilio.

Emilio pointed a finger at Théo and smiled. "Ha ha ahh ... a funny man, are you now?"

"Hello," Eloise and I said at the same time. Théo seemed like a nice enough chap, and the two men enjoyed a bit of friendly banter. I was feeling quite at home here already, knowing that we would both fit right in. Our new boss Emilio certainly seemed very pleasant.

"Now girls, first things first. What will you have to drink? Did you have breakfast yet?" Emilio reminded me of Mrs B, who was always concerned that we shouldn't get hungry or thirsty on a shift and insisted on putting us before herself and the customers. We seemed to have landed on our feet here for sure.

I looked at Eloise, knowing that Eloise especially was quite full and would have no room left for cake or anything after all the crêpes she had eaten for breakfast. "I'm OK, actually, but thank you. I'm still fit to bursting from breakfast. Our new housemate Sophia is a pastry chef, and she made a huge batch of crêpes for us before we left home."

Emilio sighed. "Ahhh, well as soon as you get

even a little bit hungry or thirsty, you be sure to tell me, alright? No good work is ever done on an empty stomach."

Chapter 9

Sébastien Paris Pâtisserie, Val D'Isera Ski
Resort, Austria: 29th November 2018

"Hello? Can I help you? I'm afraid we're not open yet. You'll have to come back later if you want to book a table." Violetta skipped swiftly across the restaurant floor towards the door, where a lady had just entered. Stefan would kill her if she didn't get the tables and chairs scrubbed and cleaned in time for the new ski season. The resort didn't officially open until the 1st December, but there was so much to do.

"I'm not here to book a table." Sophia reached out a hand to introduce herself to

Violetta, the kitchen porter. "I'm Sophia, your new head pastry chef."

"Ohhh!" Violetta exclaimed, looking confused. "But we've already employed our pastry chef for the new season. I didn't know we were getting a second one."

Sophia's heart sank. "But there must be some kind of mistake. Look, here's the letter. This *is* the Sébastien Paris Pâtisserie, *right*? I mean, I haven't walked into the wrong place by mistake? That would be a bit embarrassing?"

"I'm so sorry." Violetta thought for a second. She was sure that there wasn't a job going; Stefan hadn't mentioned anything about it. "I tell you what, why don't you sit here and I'll bring you some hot tea. Stefan, the boss, will be back soon, and then you can speak to him yourself. I've probably got it all wrong. He doesn't tell me everything, I'm just the kitchen porter."

Violetta pulled out a chair for Sophia, as she crumpled into it in a state of utter despair. The prospect of not having a job, having spent her life savings on the flight and her accommodation until her first paycheque arrived, did not sit well with her. "Thank you, Violetta, did you say your name was?"

"Yes, it's Polish."

"And you are wrong you know. There is no

such thing as *just* a kitchen porter; everyone is important in a restaurant, and without you, the pastry chef and staff would not be able to do their jobs properly, so don't ever say that you are only a kitchen porter." Sophia was empathic towards Violetta; she clearly had a hard time here, not a surprise given how fierce Michelin star restaurants could be with their staff as they strived for perfection in all aspects. Sophia should know, she'd been a kitchen porter herself all through her training, to help make ends meet. It was a thankless task.

Violetta took to Sophia instantly. If only Stefan had employed Sophia instead of that awful girl Audrey. Life had been miserable since Audrey had arrived, and the season hadn't even started yet. Things could only go from bad to worse. Violetta wondered how Audrey had passed her training course at all, as it seemed that she just gave all the work to Violetta, and if the boss didn't like what he tasted, it was Violetta who got it in the neck. Violetta poured some tea for Sophia and left to get on with her chores. "I'm so sorry, but I really must get these jobs done. Stefan is strict, and I don't want to get into trouble. But if you want someone to show you around after my shift finishes, I'd be happy to give you the grand tour.

"That's quite alright, thank you so much.

Please don't let me stop you, and yes, I'd love to have a tour, but only if you have time." Sophia stirred her tea, trying hard not to get distracted by her thoughts and the anger that was now bubbling within her. She would be gutted if the job was no longer available.

A door opened, and a cool rush of air blew across the back of Sophia's neck. It must be the boss she thought, turning around to see who had entered the room. He was a bald man with a little moustache and a round belly, and he was laughing and joking with a twenty-something lady on his arm. Sophia nearly died of shock.

Audrey recognised Sophia immediately. "Sophia? How are you? Fancy seeing you here. Didn't you get the letter about the job?"

Sophia did a double-take, not quite believing that this was happening. "You mean the letter with the job offer that I showed you at our graduation ceremony?"

Audrey laughed. "Haha. I don't recall you ever showing me a letter, Sophia dear, you must be imagining things. No, I mean the letter from Stefan and me, to say that the job was no longer available; the position had since been filled by a more suitable applicant."

"What do you mean, a *more suitable* applicant? I had the highest marks of everyone in our cohort.

I'd already accepted the job months ago. There shouldn't have been any more applicants after I'd been offered the post." Sophia was mentally thinking things through, certain that she could not have made any mistake.

"I don't know what is going on, Stefan *sweetie*, but this is Sophia, we were at culinary school together in Paris. She was always a bit delusional, but we just put it down to her growing up as an orphan. Poor thing. But I'm sure we can sort things out, can't we, darling?" Audrey pulled Stefan towards her, slipping her hand in the rear pocket of his jeans as she planted a smacker of a kiss on his lips. "Sophia, oh how rude of me. Sorry. This is my fiancée Stefan. Stefan, this is Sophia."

Sophia was stuck to the spot, motionless, her mind trying to process everything. She shook herself. "OK. So let me get this clear. I've come all the way to Austria to start this new job as Head Pastry Chef, and now *you of all people* are telling me that the job no longer exists?" Sophia waved the letter in front of her, trying to appeal to Stefan. She wasn't sure she even wanted the job if this was how things ran here, but she needed the money, and she had no plan B. How had Audrey even come to be here in the first place?

"Of course the job exists, Sophia. You really can be so *silly* sometimes, can't she, Stefan baby?"

"So there is a job for me? But I thought you just said that there wasn't?" Sophia's head was spinning.

"You don't understand, Sophia. Let me explain it in simple terms for you. Yes, there is a pastry chef job, but no, it isn't available, because the position has already been filled." Audrey shook her head at Stefan as if to point out how dim Sophia was.

"By whom? I see Violetta, and she says she is the kitchen porter, and Stefan is the boss and Head Chef ... ?" Sophia looked around her, expecting another employee to emerge from the kitchen outback.

Audrey walked towards Sophia slowly as if she were a model on a catwalk, careful to make sure that Stefan caught a full view of her tight touché. She lifted her arms gracefully and placed them on Sophia's shoulders, moving her discreetly towards the door as they spoke. "My *dear* Sophia. You are looking at *her*. I am the new Head Pastry Chef."

"You? But how can *you* be the new pastry chef? You don't even like cooking. You hate Val D'Isera because it's not posh enough, and you knew that I had already been offered the job here. It just doesn't make sense."

"Oh, come now, Sophia. No need to get so jealous. Val D'Isera has *always* been my favourite of all the ski resorts. Daddy loves it here, and why would I go to the best culinary school and waste all that time studying and working hard not to use it in one of the *best* restaurants in Europe? Hmmm. You must admit that does seem a little far-fetched. Perhaps you're tired from your flight or upset that you didn't get chosen for the job? Why don't you go and sleep it off for a bit? Calm yourself? You don't want to make a scene now, do you? I'm only saying this as your *friend*." Sophia was lost for words as she tried to fathom what Audrey was saying, but before she knew what was going on, Audrey had pushed her through the restaurant and out onto the cold street, swiftly locking the door behind her. Sophia stood dumbstruck for a moment.

"Sophia, Sophia," came a whispered voice from behind her. It was Violetta, careful not to be caught speaking to Sophia in case Audrey gave her more grief. "Sophia, I'm so sorry. If it was up to me, you'd have got the job in a heartbeat. But I can't stop. It's just ... well ... you left your coat on the chair."

"Thank you, Violetta." Sophia took the coat but did not move as Violetta hurriedly closed the door quietly behind her.

Chapter 10

Snow Mountain Cafe, Val D'Isera Ski Resort, Austria: 29th November 2018

"Energetic person. Eight letters," Théo said to the girls as he chewed on the end of the pencil, his other hand around his mug of hot coffee.

Maddy and Eloise leant forward on the coffee shop counter, thinking hard. It was only their first day on the job, but they already felt quite at home here. They just needed the tourists to arrive and create a proper buzz. For now, they had very few customers, mainly resort staff. Emilio was sitting on a reclining chair by the log fire, twanging the strings on his Spanish guitar as he played melodies from his native South America.

"I think I've got it," I announced, feeling rather proud of myself. "Go-getter."

Théo pencilled in the letters on the crossword to see if it would fit. "Yes, that's it. Well done, Maddy." Just then the coffee shop door opened, and Eloise and I stood upright, keen to make a good impression on our new customers, but we soon slouched again when we saw it was Sophia. She had lost the bounce and energy that we had seen in her this morning.

"Sophia? Is everything OK?" I asked. She looked as if she were about to cry. Emilio was quick to come to her aid and waved her in the direction of a chair by the fireplace as we gathered around her. Something seemed terribly amiss. Emilio disappeared into the kitchen to rustle up some cakes and hot chocolate and pointed Eloise and me to take a chair next to our friend so we could comfort her.

"Sophia, what's going on? You look ever so pale." Eloise patted Sophia's shoulder to comfort her, but she seemed to be in shock as she began to cry.

Sophia sniffed, trying hard to keep the tears back, but it was no use. "I just went to the restaurant to see about my new job, and they don't want me anymore."

"But why?" I asked, feeling confused. "The letter. Have you still got it? Show it to me again. They must have some legal obligation or something? Surely?"

Sophia pulled the crumpled letter from her coat pocket, and we passed it around us to be sure that we hadn't missed anything. It was clear enough. Sophia had been offered a job as Head Pastry Chef and was to show up for her first shift tonight.

Théo looked at it closely and thought for a second. "You know what?" he said. "I've heard about this Stefan guy, and he doesn't sound like a very nice person at all. Apparently, he's a bit of a womaniser; he's had several wives already, and he's only in his late thirties. Sounds like you dodged a bullet if you ask me." Théo passed the letter to Emilio, who had since returned from the kitchen with a tray of goodies for all of us to enjoy by the fire.

"Wait. Are you a pastry chef? For real?" Emilio looked stunned.

"Yes. I just qualified from St Joseph's Culinary School in Paris. I came top of my cohort as well. I worked so hard to get a place there and for the money for my fees and expenses. Now I'm unemployed, and I've spent everything I have on the chalet rental for the season."

I recognised the name from somewhere, but I couldn't think why. "Eloise, does the St Joseph's Culinary School sound familiar to you?" Eloise nodded in agreement.

"What an absolute idiot, to let someone like you go. It seems ridiculous. St Joseph's Culinary School is one of the best in the world, and if you say that you came top of your year, then you really must be good. I can't believe that anyone in their right mind would not hire you. It's just crazy." Emilio seemed horrified at such a thought.

"Hey, wait! Didn't you say that you wanted to employ a pot washer, Emilio? You know, for when Maddy and I bring in all these new customers?" Eloise had come up with an idea. I could tell by the glint in her eye.

Emilio seemed confused but interested to hear more. "Well, yes, I certainly would like to employ a pot washer, but I don't see how that would help Sophia? A person with her qualifications should be earning a lot more money than I could afford."

Eloise looked in the direction of Sophia, who was now wiping her nose with a napkin that Théo had found for her. "Look, I know it's not the job that you wanted to be doing, but didn't you tell us that you worked as a kitchen porter during your holidays?"

"Umm, yes," Sophia replied. "Well, then, since Emilio needs a pot washer and you need a job, why don't you come and work here? At least it would be something, a start, take the pressure off for a while until you can find a pastry chef job somewhere." Eloise was gentle with Sophia.

Emilio looked sad. "Eloise is right. It *would* be something, even if it was just to tide you over. I'm only sorry that I can't pay you more. The money isn't much; we simply don't have enough customers right now, but I could give you the freedom of the kitchen to bake whenever and whatever you wanted with the supplies I have in the storeroom."

"No, no, that would be *amazing*. It would be a great help, and I think I'd much rather work here anyway, having seen how horrid the conditions were at the restaurant." Sophia smiled through her tears, touched at the kindness of her new friends.

"Seriously? You would wash pots for us at our little cafe?" Emilio couldn't believe his luck. He had always dreamed of the cafe one day offering the best cakes and pastries, but he didn't think in a million years that he would have a trained pastry chef in his kitchen. "Actually, I tell you what. If the four of us can get the cafe bringing in more customers and enough money to cover the wages of a pastry chef over the winter season, then I will promote you to Head Pastry Chef of the Snow Mountain Cafe. How about that?"

It sounded like a wonderful plan and a nice challenge as far as I was concerned. Eloise had come up with an idea that would work for all of us, and Emilio even said that if we brought in more business, he would give Eloise and me a pay increase too, which would mean more money for our detective agency in the long term.

"Well, I'll raise my mug of hot chocolate to that!" I said as I lifted it the air. But the mood was not yet improved.

"There's something else." Sophia looked hesitant like she had a horrid, deep dark secret that could ruin everything in a second. "The thing is, what I don't understand is that the job was mine. I applied for it, did the interview over Skype, sent references and everything, and the reason I didn't get the job was that someone else had been offered it. A girl who was on the course with me. I told her about my new job when we were at our graduation ceremony, and she didn't once mention that she had plans to work here, which is weird. She was supposed to be going to St Tropez for the summer, and then her dad was going to buy her a restaurant in Paris. So I just don't understand why she is here at all."

Eloise and I spat out our hot chocolates at the same moment. "Wait. Did you say, St Tropez?" I asked.

"Yes. Her dad is a billionaire, and she never once showed interest in actually working as a pastry chef." Sophia was trying to fathom things as Eloise and I suddenly looked at each other.

"Well, well, this does seem odd. Maddy, what was the name of that horrible girl your mother introduced us to at the summer party? Amanda? Amelia? Aud—"

Eloise did not need to finish her sentence; we both suddenly recalled the girl's name and *why* the name of the culinary school sounded familiar. "Audrey Flandin!" we said in unison. Sophia went suddenly pale and limp. It certainly seemed like an odd coincidence to come across the same Audrey.

Théo rushed to Sophia's side and held her up in her chair as Emilio wafted Théo's newspaper to create some air around her. Sophia was very pasty, and it took a few moments for her to come to. Emilio got her a glass of tap water from the kitchen, and Théo helped her take small sips as she recovered herself. "I'm so sorry," she said. "But you gave me quite a fright."

Sophia told us everything, about how Audrey borrowed the culinary kit she had worked and saved so hard for, and how she had bullied her in class and made the other students do all the work for her. It seemed to fit with the Audrey that Eloise and I had met at that summer party in August.

"So, you girls know this Audrey too, then?" Théo asked us.

"Yes," Eloise replied, moving her leg away from the fire, which was getting quite hot against her winter boots. "Well, I think 'know her' might be a bit strong, but we met her once at a party, and she was the ghastliest person I've ever met. Don't you agree, Maddy?"

"Absolutely. And the weirdest thing is, I distinctly remember how she scoffed at us when we told her that we were coming to Val D'Isera for the ski season. I'm pretty sure that she said we *wouldn't catch her dead coming to a place like this*," I added.

Eloise added more as she remembered fragments of our only encounter with Audrey. "'*Full of commoners and nouveau riche*' was how she described this place if I remember rightly?"

"She sounds like a not very nice person at all if you ask me." Théo somehow seemed to lift Sophia's spirits, helped further by some words of encouragement from Emilio.

"Well, it seems to me that fate did not intend for you to waste your youth in that hell hole, and instead you will be very welcomed into our little family here at the Snow Mountain Café. If that Audrey ever shows her face here, then we'll be only too happy to sort her out for you."

Chapter 11

Ski Chalet, Val D'Isera Ski Resort, Austria: 29th November 2018

"Hey, ladies. So how did your first day go? Was it all that you hoped it would be?" Nicklas Rehn poured them shots to toast their first day at the resort. He was a rather handsome, blonde-haired, blue-eyed ski instructor from Sweden, who was, luckily for Madeleine, Eloise, and Sophia, their housemate, along with his fraternal twin Karl.

"OMG! You wouldn't *believe* the day we've had," I said, taking one of the glasses and knocking it back in a single mouthful. I wasn't one for drinking alcohol, but since it was a special occasion, I decided to enjoy the purple-coloured kirsch liquor. It was warming as it ran down my throat. It seemed like a long time ago that we had been stood here in the kitchen eating crêpes with Sophia for breakfast.

"Really? I always thought Emilio seemed like a lovely guy to work for." Nicklas was very surprised.

"Oh no," I replied. "Emilio is awesome and the café is lush. Eloise and I had a brilliant day, but poor Sophia had a rather horrid time at her new job."

"Why? What happened?" Nicklas looked at Sophia with genuine concern. She had already been very supportive, even helping him to start his car this morning with jump leads before breakfast.

Sophia was quiet, too traumatised to talk about the events of the day, so she let Eloise do the explaining for her. "Yes, poor Sophia. Turns out that her boss Stefan had gone and given her job to someone else. So now Sophia is working with us in the coffee shop. Emilio gave her the coolest work though, and now she'll be the cafe's head chef and can bake anything at all that she wants. Emilio says that if we all bring in extra customers and money, then we'll get a pay rise too. So it all worked out in the end. Pretty good for a first day on the job, eh? The pay rise I mean, obviously not the Sophia part. That part just sucks."

"That's awful." Nicklas looked at Sophia as she averted her gaze; she was understandably distressed by the whole turn of events.

"Now that you mention it, I did hear something about a new girl starting there. I just assumed that the boss was hiring more chefs this year. My girlfriend Violetta works there as a kitchen porter, but we hardly ever get to hang out since the new girl started. She sounds like a right cow from what Violetta has told me. Violetta was supposed to get a promotion so that she could start baking more and work up to one day being Head Chef, but when the new girl started, she didn't get the promotion she was promised."

I punched Nicklas in a friendly way on his arm. "Why didn't you mention this earlier? At least Sophia would have been prepared before her first shift?"

Nicklas shrugged his shoulders. "I don't know. I suppose I just didn't want you all to be disappointed. You were so excited this morning, and maybe it would have been different for you working as a pastry chef, having a bit more status than a kitchen porter, I mean. Did you meet Violetta by any chance?"

Sophia looked embarrassed. Not exactly the way she wanted to start her new life, being made to look stupid in front of everyone. "Yes, I did meet Violetta and she was lovely. Really kind, as it happens. I just felt bad for her, as they didn't seem like decent people to work for. If it wasn't for Violetta, I wouldn't have got my coat or purse back, because Audrey threw me out of the restaurant and locked the door behind me. Thankfully, Violetta handed my coat to me afterwards, and my purse was still in the pocket. But I did lose my scarf, hat, and gloves. Maybe if you see Violetta, you could ask her to give them to you so I can get them back? If you don't mind, of course?"

"Yeah, no problem at all. I'm seeing her later, so I'll ask her to bring them along when she finishes her shift."

Chapter 12

Disco Diva Bar and Club, Val D'Isera Ski Resort, Austria: 29th November 2018

"Hey, you." Nicklas kissed Violetta on the cheek and pulled out a bar stool for her. She looked exhausted. "Drink?"

Violetta stared at the optics on the wall behind the bar. All she wanted was a cup of hot chamomile tea and an early night, but since she was in the bar of the club, the options were nowhere near her drink of choice. "Just a lime and soda, thanks. I can't stay for long; I've got work in the morning. Audrey has me prepping for her again. Honestly, I've never met anyone so lazy. I swear she thinks I'm her servant."

A ginger headed young man with freckles

tidied away some glasses on a shelf. "Alright, bro? What can I get you?" It was Nicklas's brother Karl, the club's bartender. He was not at all sporty, unlike Nicklas, and he wasn't a fan of the great outdoors.

"Lime and soda for Violetta, and a beer for me. Thanks, Karl." Nicklas and Karl grabbed each other's arms, like two gangster rappers with a secret handshake.

"How's life with the devil lady?" Karl asked Violetta, an air of cheekiness about him.

Violetta tensed, pounding her fist into the palm of her hand. "Oh … don't get me started. It's Violetta this and Violetta that, and she goes on and on about her rich father. I don't think she's ever done a proper day's work in her life."

Karl popped the lid on the bottle of beer and poured it into a glass. "I don't suppose there's much point in talking to Stefan about things, is there? I mean, I heard nice things about him last season, before this Audrey arrived. It's not fair the way she has you running around after her; you get paid a fraction of what she does, yet it seems like you are the one doing all the work?" Karl shook his head from side to side in annoyance.

"I know, right?" Violetta took a sip from her glass. "I thought I'd at least get a little bit of time off to go skiing, but even when I do, I'm too exhausted to even eat. It's crazy! I swear I'll end up killing her before the season is out." Violetta laughed at herself and how animated she had become at the mere mention of Audrey's name.

"Well, babe, if *you* don't kill her, then *I* certainly will. I can't have her stealing my girl and making her so exhausted all the time." Nicklas kissed Violetta on the hand and gave her a loving look.

Karl pretended to vomit. "Aww, get a room, you guys."

"No, but seriously, today she was doubly weird. I had a bad feeling, but I can't explain why. This girl called Sophia was supposed to have gotten the job as Head Pastry Chef, and she turned up today with this letter saying that she should come to start her shift this evening. But when Stefan and Audrey got there, they denied it all. Stefan didn't seem to know anything about her being offered a job, and Audrey said that the job was already hers. I mean, she *literally* threw Sophia out the door, onto the cold street; wouldn't even let me open the door to give the girl her coat back."

Karl and Nicklas listened closely. It certainly sounded strange, and from having met their new housemate Sophia, they were surprised that anyone would want to be nasty to her; she seemed like a lovely person. Happy go lucky, wouldn't harm a fly. Nicklas suddenly remembered about Sophia's scarf. "That reminds me, Sophia left her hat, gloves, and scarf behind at the restaurant. Any chance you can get them for me? I don't think Sophia's got a lot of money, especially now she's had to get a job as a pot washer at the Snow Mountain Café. I'm sure it'll cheer her up to get them back."

Violetta picked some fluff from Nicklas's fleece top and leant her hand on his shoulder. "Sure. I would have given them to her earlier, but it was hard enough sneaking out her coat with Stefan and Audrey hanging around. I thought they might fire me on the spot if they caught me helping her. But I only saw a hat and scarf, unless the gloves had fallen somewhere. I'll have a proper look tomorrow."

"Thanks, babe." Nicklas smiled at Violetta, clearly smitten.

"Anyway, bro? What's new with you? I've hardly seen you, what with you working nights and me working days." Nicklas turned his attention to Karl, who was busy slicing up lemons.

"Yeah. All good with me. I got a letter from Miryam this morning. She sends you her love." Karl looked up momentarily as the juice from a lemon irritated a small cut on his finger.

"Oh yeah? How's she getting on? Has she got herself a job yet or is she still wheeling and dealing? Honestly, I don't know why you bother keeping in touch with her; she's a slippery one." Nicklas seemed a bit rattled by the conversation. He was not a fan of his thieving cousin Miryam Löfgren, but at least she was in Sweden and far enough away from Karl to not lead him into trouble with the law. She'd never actually done anything to harm either of them, and they rubbed along fine, but something about her rang alarm bells with Nicklas, and he was concerned at how trusting Karl seemed to be when it came to her, even though she was family.

"I take it you are not keen on this Miryam, then Nicklas?" Violetta asked.

"No, I'm not," Nicklas replied. "I mean, she's nice enough, don't get me wrong, but I just think she's too focused on earning an easy buck, and I doubt she would stop at anything to make it happen. I just don't trust her. I don't know. I can't explain it; it's just a feeling I have, ever since we were kids and she made Karl steal sweets from our grandma so she could sell them and make money for herself. She even let Karl take the rap for it."

Violetta nodded. It was surprising for Nicklas not to be keen on anyone. He was one of the few people she knew who always saw the good in people.

Violetta knocked back her lime and soda water and declared it a night. "I'm sorry, guys, but I really, really need my bed. I've got to be up again at 4 am, and I don't want to give Audrey any more reasons to shout at me. No, no, you stay here, Nicklas. No need to come with me; I'll be fine to get home. See you later, Karl."

Chapter 13

Snow Mountain Café, Val D'Isera Ski Resort,
Austria: 30th November 2018

"What's it like in South America, Emilio?" I asked, keen to learn more about my new boss.

"Well, where I come from, it's a little village and a bit dull, but in the rainforests, there are monkeys and puma, and the noise is so incredible. It's the loudest place on earth. I try to go back whenever I can." I hung on to every word that Emilio spoke; he seemed to have led a rich and exciting life, and he knew so much about the world.

"Where's the most exciting place you've ever been to?" Eloise asked as she rolled out the puff pastry. The coffee shop was empty apart from Théo, who was busy with his crossword in the daily newspaper, so Sophia gave Eloise, Emilio, and me an impromptu lesson in baking.

"That's a tough question to answer. I think every place I go to is the best place in the world. At least until I go to the next new place, anyway." Emilio laughed at himself. "Last year I thought that the Galapagos was the best place ever, but then this summer, I travelled all across Asia, and it was magical." Emilio's expression told us that he was already reminiscing over his summer exploits.

"Wow. I hope that I get to go travelling when I'm older." I sighed, feeling like I wasn't a proper grown-up yet.

"What do you mean?" Eloise laughed at me. "You are travelling and having great adventures already. You *are* in Austria, don't forget, and you've never been *here* before. OK, it might be closer to home than Peru or Brazil, and far less exciting or exotic than Egypt, but it is still travel." Eloise turned her pastry over and dusted the surface with some flour. "What about you, Sophia; have you travelled much?"

Sophia's eyes looked sad. "Me? Oh no, I've

hardly travelled at all. I've only been to France, mostly Paris, and, well, now here."

Eloise did her best to cheer Sophia up. "I'm fairly sure that's all about to change, a famous pastry chef like you. You'll soon be off gallivanting and collecting recipes from far and wide and publishing them in shiny-covered hardback books for your *adoring* fans."

The four of us giggled at the thought, and Emilio said that he was just so excited to know that everything had all begun in his tiny kitchen. He hoped we three girls would not forget him when we were rich and famous.

Sophia turned to Emilio. "But in all seriousness, I'd love to hear more about Asia. Have you been before?"

"Oh yes, I've been many times, to different places. I travel every holiday as much as I can. I'm a bit of a geek, you see. I like to collect different coffee and cocoa beans. I'll show you my collection if you like." Emilio was quite taken at how interested the girls were in his travels. He'd always felt a bit lonely before, with no one to share his adventures and collection of beans with.

"Seriously? You've got a bean collection?" Sophia seemed surprised.

"I know it doesn't sound very cool, does it?

But my collection is very special in my eyes." Emilio looked a little wounded.

It wasn't what Sophia had meant at all, and she seemed genuinely animated by the whole prospect of beans from around the world. "You misunderstand me, Emilio. I think *you* are the most incredible person I have *ever* met. I've always wanted to do something similar, to have my own collection of ingredients. I just never imagined that I would meet someone who shared my passion for beans and flavours."

Emilio grabbed Sophia's and my arms and escorted the three of us to follow him into the storeroom. He pushed a metal shelf away from the wall and entered some numbers into a security pad.

"Umm, Emilio?" I gasped, totally in awe of what I saw before me. "Are you telling us that you have a walk-in safe and it is full of beans? *And* secret?"

Eloise was as astonished as I was. "Whoa, you *actually* have a secret room in your coffee shop? That is the most brilliant thing I ever saw. You are like a real-life Jack, like Jack and the Beanstalk, except that your beans aren't magic …obviously."

Emilio smiled and led them into a large cupboard. "Well, I suppose in some ways the beans could be said to be magic. I mean, this one here will perk you up, this one will help you with memory, and this one here will kill you in an instant. This one is not really a bean, but a seed that I picked up in Asia, and although the outside of the fruit can be eaten, the inner part is toxic and will kill you very painfully in less than an hour."

I looked around the room at all the wonderful glass jars on every shelf. It was a very large collection. "Oh, so that's why you need to keep them in a safe then?" I theorised.

"It's more that I don't want anyone to steal them. I'd be mortified after years of collecting them on my travels." Emilio handed a jar to Sophia so that she could examine the contents.

"I've read about some of these," Sophia said, looking closer at the white label on a large glass jar. "May I?"

"Of course," Emilio replied as Sophia unscrewed the lid and pulled out one of the beans. "I think I've just found heaven. I could make so many things from these ingredients, *if* you would permit me to, of course?"

Emilio hesitated for a second, unsure if he was ready to part with his prized bean collection. "We'll see. I'm sure I could spare one or two, but I'd hate to use up all the beans, as some of them are now extinct. I'm hoping to plant them one day when I've got a garden anyway."

Sophia handed the jar back to Emilio as Théo announced from the front of the shop that they finally had a customer.

Chapter 14

Snow Mountain Café, Val D'Isera Ski Resort, Austria: 30th November 2018

"I don't believe it. What is she doing here? Such a nerve." Eloise recognised Audrey from their first meeting at the summer party. She had entered the coffee shop with two older women, and they were having an unpleasant conversation in French.

"Maddy, come here a minute!" Eloise called me over, and I, too, was surprised to see Audrey at the café. Surely, the word must have reached her by now about Sophia's new place of employment.

Audrey and the two women approached the counter. "Haven't we met before?" I asked Audrey, knowing full well that we had met at the summer party just a few months earlier.

"I *don't* think so." Audrey declared, giving me a filthy look. I only hoped that Sophia did not catch her here.

"What can I get you?" Eloise asked with a firm but far more professional voice than I could bring myself to use.

"Three espressos and whatever those cakes are, though they look like they've seen better days. Very amateur indeed, not like the fine pastries we have at our restaurant, that's for sure." Audrey pointed a stubby, manicured finger at the freshly made cakes. They looked stunning to everyone but Audrey.

I grabbed three small plates and plonked the cakes onto them with as little care as possible. The cakes were wasted on someone who clearly would not appreciate them.

"Bring them over, will you; we'll see if we can find a *clean* table somewhere." Audrey was unnecessarily rude, and she certainly wasn't winning us over with her attitude.

"What does she mean '*clean* table?'" I hissed at Eloise once Audrey was out of earshot. "The tables are immaculate."

"Just ignore her. She's trying to wind you up, Maddy."

"Well, it's working," I said with a huff.

I marched over to the table and left the coffees and cakes in front of the three women, my eye spotting some interesting paperwork in the process. I was glad that I had studied A-Level French at sixth form. I went back to the counter and picked up a fresh cloth.

"There's something strange going on at the table. There are loads of legal documents. I'm going to pretend to clean the tables again, seeing as they are so *filthy*. Maybe I can pick up something from their conversation, find out what they are up to." I told Eloise.

"Good idea, Maddy." Eloise gave me the thumbs up just as Emilio emerged from the kitchen.

Emilio watched me with the cloth. "Everything OK?" he asked.

"I'll let Eloise explain," I said as I sidled off to a table close enough to hear what Audrey was talking about.

Eloise signalled for Emilio to come over to a quiet corner of the coffee shop, away from Sophia. "Emilio, may I have a word? That's Audrey," she whispered. "The girl who stole the job from Sophia. She seems to be up to something. Maddy's going to try and listen in, but

Sophia mustn't see Audrey here; it will only upset her."

Emilio nodded that he understood. "Sure thing. She's certainly been through enough hurt lately; no need to upset her further."

Emilio went back into the kitchen and Eloise busied herself with Théo and his latest crossword, leaving me to eavesdrop on whatever it was that Audrey was up to.

"Audrey, it's very important that you sign these documents, especially now that you are engaged to be married. I just need your signature here, here, *and* here. Then I'll be able to head back to Paris and leave you in peace." From what I could understand from their conversation and my quick scan of the paperwork, the elder of the two women was called Margot Baillieu-Flandin, and she was Audrey's stepmother. Audrey was keen enough to sign, but the other woman, who was slightly younger, and much more plain-looking, kept interrupting them.

"Are you sure you want to sign, Audrey? Don't you want to read through the small print first? This is a great deal of money, after all, and it's going to be yours as soon as you are married or when you reach your next birthday, whichever comes first. I'd hate for you to sign your life away." The plain-looking lady, who went by the name of

Rose Landry, seemed quiet and timid, especially compared to Audrey and Margot.

Margot looked cross. "Oh, for goodness sake, Rose. Will you stop mithering the girl? I'm sure she knows her own mind by now. She doesn't *need* you interfering. She gets enough of that from her father without you joining in."

Rose lowered her half-moon glasses on her nose and looked Margot straight in the eyes. "With all due respect, Margot, I'm here because Audrey's father sent me to make sure that she knows *what* she is signing. He simply wants the *best* for his daughter. As do I!"

Audrey had heard enough from the two women, and stood up to leave, knocking her coffee slightly so that the liquid spilt over the papers. "I tell you what, why don't the two of you come back to me when you've settled your argument, or better still, you can just leave me in peace." Audrey grabbed her handbag and stormed out of the coffee shop, leaving the two women to sort out the papers which had blown off the table as the wind caught the coffee shop door.

"So, what did you find out?" Emilio asked.

I wasn't sure what I had found out, to be honest, or how it was relevant. "It seems that Audrey is about to inherit a large sum of money as soon as she marries or reaches her next birthday. The larger of the ladies is called Margot and is Audrey's stepmother, and the thinner of the two ladies is Rose Landry, who works as a secretary for Audrey's father, Felix."

"And did she sign the papers?" Eloise asked me.

"No, she got fed up with the two women fighting, so she stormed out. But *my* guess is that the stepmother wants her to sign the papers, but her father's secretary does not." I was yet to find a logical explanation for why one lady wanted Audrey to sign, and the other did not, but I'd need more information first. I didn't get an opportunity to think about things further, as Sophia called me from the kitchen to tell me my bakes had finished cooking.

Part Four

A Glacier Visit

Part Four

A Glorior Night

Chapter 15

Ski Chalet, Val D'Isera Ski Resort, Austria: 1st December 2018

Nicklas looked like an excited schoolboy at Christmas, his face dazzling with enthusiasm. "Honestly, Maddy, you should see the glacier; it's *so* beautiful. I can't wait to show it to you."

I zipped up my boots and threw on my padded down jacket. "I can see that," I laughed. His enthusiasm was contagious. It was the first official day of the winter ski season, and the first flights filled with skiers, all set for their holiday, would be arriving later in the afternoon. It was our last chance to explore the resort before things became busy and the resort heaving with holidaymakers.

Nicklas had decided to have a dry run of his glacier tour to get him in the swing of things before the guests arrived, and he opened the trip to the staff and people already on the resort. Emilio had given us the morning off since the coffee shop was now well and truly stocked with coffee and freshly baked cakes ready for the first customers later in the day. He assured us that he could manage quite well with his one main customer, Théo, all on his own. I'd never seen a glacier before and I was struggling to decide what to wear.

"I'd better get going," Nicklas announced. "I need to be at the coach to meet the driver before everyone arrives."

"No worries. We'll see you there in a bit," I said, waving Nicklas off as he sped towards the door.

"Do you think I'll be warm enough?" I asked Sophia as I wrapped a long scarf around my neck and tucked my mittens in my jacket pocket.

"Yes, I'm sure you'll be fine. You just need a jacket, salopettes, boots, hat, gloves, and a scarf. Anyway, I don't think we'll be up there too long, and the walk will soon warm us up if it gets cold." Sophia was reassuring as ever. Eloise and I found ourselves seeking her advice on things. She was clever, and most importantly, she was patient with us, especially when teaching us how to bake more sophisticated cakes and pastries. We would have a lot of new skills to share with Mrs B when we got back to Mrs Tiggywinkle's and worked our coffee shop shifts once we started university.

"I've got some spare gloves if you want to borrow them," Eloise offered, knowing that Sophia's had gone missing the day she had been thrown out of the restaurant by Audrey.

"Oh no, I couldn't. I'd be afraid I might lose them. I've got lovely warm pockets anyway." Sophia was strong-willed, and it seemed that once she had made her mind up about not accepting help, there was nothing we could do to change it. "Thanks anyway, though. That's sweet of you."

Eloise was just as stubborn. "I tell you what; I'll pack them in my rucksack, and that way, if you change your mind, I've got them. How about that?"

Sophia nodded her head. "Sure."

I fastened my rucksack and put it on my back. It was heavier than I had planned, but I figured that wouldn't be a bad thing, given how many cakes and pastries I had eaten in one week. I'd have to get a lot of exercise if I wanted to avoid going home twice my current size. "Right, I think

I'm all set. We should probably get a wriggle on. We said we would meet Nicklas at the coach by 9 am, and it's already close to that."

"Holy Moly!" Eloise replied, throwing on her rucksack and doing up the buckles. The three of us hurried through the door and walked as quickly as we could through the town to the ski shop, ready to meet Nicklas.

Chapter 16

Ski Shop, Val D'Isera Ski Resort, Austria: 1st December 2018

"All set, Nicklas?" Daan asked with a cheery smile.

"Hey, dude! How're things?" Nicklas high-fived Daan van Bree, the ski shop's Dutch technician. He'd been off on expedition over the summer and looked like he'd burnt up a lot of calories. "How was the Arctic?"

"Buddy, it was incredible. We kite-skied right up to the North Pole. Best trip ever."

"Whoa! That sounds rad." Nicklas found himself staring at the funny white circles around

Daan's eyes where his sunglasses had been. He looked like a tan and white panda.

"So, what do you need from me today? Any kit or supplies?" Daan waved in the general direction of the rental gear and emergency kit for the instructors and rescue teams.

"Nah, I think I'm alright, thanks, but I'll point the group in your general direction, in case they need anything." Nicklas looked around the shop, his eyes bulging at all the new ski lines hanging from the rails. He wished he had more money so he could buy some of the new clothing.

"Don't forget to tell them about the staff discount, in case they want to use it themselves. They can pick up their staff ski passes here too." Daan was always keen to get more people out and about on the slopes.

"Awesome." Nicklas pulled out his phone to check the time. The coach and group would be arriving soon. His brother was supposed to be here by now. Said he had wanted to earn a bit of extra cash by helping Nicklas to tick off the guests on his clipboard list as they arrived. "Don't suppose you've seen that brother of mine, have you?"

Daan shook his head, then pointed at the shop door. "Ahh, there he is, late as ever. Hangover, Karl?"

Karl walked through the shop with a bit of a lazy swag. "No way, dude. I don't get hangovers. Hangovers are for wimps." He gave Daan a manly hug and high-fived Nicklas.

"Daan, can you sort Karl out with some kit? You know what these indoor folks are like. Don't get outdoors much and go all flaky soon as they see a snowflake." Nicklas pulled Karl into a brotherly-love headlock and ruffled his hair.

"Girlfriend not coming?" Karl asked Nicklas.

"Nah, chance would be a fine thing. She'd have been here in a flash, but she's got to do all the work for Stefan and Audrey. The cheek of them! It's alright for them to take time off, but then they just pile the work on Violetta. It wouldn't be so bad, but Violetta's got a nasty cold. She should be home resting." Nicklas looked irritated.

"Man, that sucks." Karl shook his head in disgust.

Daan returned from the storage area weighed down with a pile of clothing. "Here we go. This should fit you, Karl."

Karl grabbed the clothing from Daan. "Cheers, buddy."

Chapter 17

Glacier Excursion, Val D'Isera Ski Resort,
Austria: 1st December 2018

"Right. Is everyone here? For those of you who don't know me, my name is Nicklas Rehn. I'm a ski guide here at Val D'Isera, and today I'm going to be your guide as we visit the glacier. I'll be giving you more details as we approach our destination. But for now, all you need to do is to sit back and relax."

"He's ever so professional, isn't he?" I remarked to Eloise.

"And handsome too. His girlfriend was lucky to snag him," Eloise giggled, her face flushing red.

"What? Do you fancy him then?" It was

always fun to tease Eloise, especially since she embarrassed easily.

The coach was already full, and only a few spaces remained. Since Eloise and I sat together, Sophia was left to sit on her own, a spare seat next to her close to the aisle. There were just two seats left now.

"Ahh, here they are at last, our two stragglers. I think there are spaces for you in the middle of the coach there." Nicklas pointed the two passengers to the remaining seats.

I was horrified and I felt for Sophia. The remaining passengers, Audrey and Stefan, took their seats. Audrey sat next to Sophia and Stefan across the aisle. They were still holding hands and insisted on French kissing for most of the journey. Sophia seemed to take it well, considering. She stared out of the window, arms folded across her chest, her body as far away from Audrey as she could manage. Eloise and I shared concerned glances, not knowing what to do to ease her discomfort.

I elbowed Eloise gently in the side. "Look over there. Do you see them?"

Eloise looked confused. "See who? What is it I'm supposed to be looking at?" She surveyed the general direction of my nod. "Oooh, I see. You mean the two French women from the coffee shop?" Eloise commented.

"Yes, exactly!" I watched the two women for much of the short coach journey. They had clearly chosen to travel together and go on the excursion, stuck to each other like glue, yet they didn't seem to be especially fond of each other or have anything in common. They barely spoke other than to argue. I didn't catch a great deal of their conversation, but I did pick up the words 'papers', 'sign', 'come of age', and 'inheritance.'

I turned to Eloise. "They seem to be still arguing about those papers I saw at the coffee shop, but I'm pretty sure they aren't even friends, so it must be to do with Audrey's trust fund?"

Eloise looked at me as if remembering some useful piece of information. "Oh yeah. Do you remember when we first met her at the summer party? She said something then about her getting a load of money as soon as she married or reached her next birthday. It has to be to do with that. But why would her stepmother want her to sign papers? Why would she be so interested? It doesn't seem like she and Audrey are that close."

I thought for a moment, processing what Eloise said. "Well, I think we should try and speak to them during the excursion, see if we can find out any more."

Eloise shook my hand. "Agreed."

A finger tapped on a microphone over the loudspeaker, the voice of Nicklas blaring through the speakers. "OK, folks. If you look out of the window to your left, you will see the glacier above you. There are two types of glaciers on the planet; the alpine glacier and the continental ice sheet. This one here is an alpine glacier. The ice is hundreds of thousands of years old, and the blue colour you will see once we get close to it is caused by the ice being dense and compact. Glaciers are basically huge masses of fallen snow that have been compressed to form ice and now flow like a slow-moving river. In a moment, we'll be stopping in the lay-by, ready to begin our walk, and I recommend that you *don't* put all your layers of clothing on at once, even if you feel cold at the start. That's because you will get very *hot* as we walk up the short but steep slope, and if you get sweaty, that sweat will cool once we stop on the glacier and could lead to hypothermia. Is everyone clear on that?"

A unanimous "yeah" ran through the coach as people started doing up boot laces and preparing themselves for the trek. Nicklas continued with his safety briefing.

"Now, if you follow my instructions, you will be perfectly safe, but you should not,

110

under *any* circumstances, go off on your own. Doing so will put yourself and the rest of us in great danger. You must follow me as we walk across the glacier. Do not go off on your own path, as there are deep crevasses and you could easily fall down them. It's a very long way down. There is no guarantee that anyone will be able to rescue you, should you fall down a crevasse, so please, please, *please* follow my instructions. That is why I have spent years training as a mountain guide, and I have amassed many, many hours as a guide here. Is everybody clear?"

There was another drawl of "yes" from the passengers as the reality of the glacier walk sank in.

The coach pulled in to the lay-by, and Karl ticked off the names of each each person as they climbed down the steps and onto the ground. There was a huge sense of anticipation, excitement, and nerves now, and the passengers were packing and repacking and double-checking their backpacks.

"By Jove, this is exciting." Eloise beamed at me as we climbed off the bus and out into the cool, clean air of the mountain.

I could barely speak during the ascent, partly due to the slight change in altitude, but mostly down to Nicklas being right about the slope being steep at first. It was as much as I could do to put one ski boot in front of the other as my heavy legs swung in front of me and settled into the snow. It didn't take long to reach the glacier, and the ground flattened off as we reached its side. Nicklas led us across the surface as we followed him in a neat line, like ants on a march. No one dared step away from his tracks in the snow. Finally, we reached the other side, and Nicklas led us up into a magnificent ice cave.

"Whoa!" was the reaction of every one of us as we entered a magnificent blue room. Nicklas was not wrong when he said that I would love it.

"OK, guys. We're going to stop here for a bit for some lunch and time for you to take photos. You can walk around in here and just outside the entrance, but don't go wandering off, unless of course, you want to die." Nicklas laughed playfully as the party of people joined in nervously.

"Come on," Audrey said as she pulled Stefan over to the wall of ice. "This would make a great selfie." She pulled out her iPhone and positioned it for maximum effect. Afterwards, she slipped it back into her pocket as she grabbed Stefan for yet another kiss.

"I *really* don't see what Audrey finds so attractive about him," Sophia remarked, watching the two lovers embrace by the wall of ice. "I mean, he's almost old enough to be her father, he's practically bald, *and* he's got a pot belly."

Audrey noticed Sophia staring at her kissing Stefan. "Seriously, Sophia, what is your problem with us? Are you jealous? Why are you even here, not just on this trip, but here in Austria? I swear, it's like you fancy me or something, like you are stalking me. Face it, honey, I'm just not into you."

It was a good thing that the excursion was only for the resort staff. Otherwise, it would have been awful for Nicklas if there were real, paying guests in the coach party. I looked at Eloise and then at Sophia. Audrey didn't need to speak to Sophia like that, and in front of everyone. Sophia looked humiliated and stormed out of the cave for a moment. She looked like she was about to cry.

"Sophia!" I called out, chasing to catch her up before she left the cave.

Sophia patted my arm. "It's alright. I'll be fine in a minute. I'm just going to get some fresh air. I'll be back in a bit."

"OK." I offered. "Just don't go off on your own, alright? Audrey's not worth it. We all know what she's like."

Eloise caught up with me and handed me a chocolate muffin. "I hope Sophia's going to be alright. You know, maybe we should talk to Audrey, ask her to lay off Sophia. They can't keep on at each other like this. It's not good for anyone, and it'll be awful if they behave like this with the tourists around."

"Hmm, I think you're right," I replied, though I wasn't convinced that someone as mean as Audrey would care about the feelings of another. But someone needed to stop them from fighting.

"Here, why don't you take her one of Emilio's doughnuts as a kind of peace offering?" Eloise passed me a paper bag of red velvet doughnuts. Audrey was sure to complain about them, but it was the best we could do on short notice.

I walked over to Audrey, who was now sitting on Stefan's knee, stroking his hair in the back of the ice cave. The sight was sickening, but I needed to be strong.

"Here, I've brought you some of our doughnuts, in case you're still hungry. I'd really like to speak with you in private, Audrey, just for a minute. Can we go outside for a bit?" I gave the doughnuts to Stefan and waited for Audrey to follow me. I didn't think for a moment that she would, but she surprised me as she stood up and led the way to the outside of the cave. I could feel my hands trembling.

Audrey walked underneath a ledge on the outside of the cave, into a little nook where we would have some privacy. She pulled out a tissue and blew her nose.

Audrey rubbed her hand on my arm gently as a tear rolled down her cheeks. I thought it must have been from the cold at first, but I suddenly realised that she was crying, and her eyes were filled with pain and sadness. "Look, I'm sorry, OK?" Audrey divulged, knocking me for six. I'd expected a lot of different reactions to my request to speak to her in private, but this was not one of them. "It's just, well, it's complicated, you see. Sophia had a bit of a thing for me at culinary school, and she didn't take it at all well when I turned her down. She just wouldn't accept it. And now she seems to follow me wherever I am and does everything she can to turn people against me. She did it in college too. That's why I was so mysterious when you asked me about my plans for the summer and for the future." Audrey wiped her eyes with the tips of her fingers as more tears streamed down her face. She was very convincing, but something was bothering me.

There was one glaringly obvious hole in this sob story; I simply had to ask her for more information. What kind of detective would I be if I didn't quiz her for details? "I see. But why did you think that we would tell Sophia about your plans? We didn't even know Sophia back then."

Audrey cleared her throat. "It was when you said that you'd got the job at the coffee shop at this exact resort. It seemed too much of a coincidence that we should be working in the same place, and I knew that if Sophia found out that I would be working here, she would follow me, and chances were you would meet her, and then she would spread her lies about me. I'm not a bad person, you know. It's just that Sophia has made me a bit paranoid, put me on edge, and it comes across as me being snooty, but that's just not who I am." Audrey's story did seem a little plausible, but I was confused about the situation with the job offer.

It was make-or-break time, and I needed answers. "But what about the letter that Sophia has, the job offer from Stefan? It looks pretty genuine."

Audrey hesitated for a second but hid it well, pretending to cry again. I was starting to doubt my own gut instinct. She was very convincing, but so was Sophia. Audrey coughed into her tissue. "Look, Madeleine. There's something that you don't understand about Sophia. She's not the person you think she is. She's manipulative and devious. You know her parents died, don't you?"

"Um, yes," I said

"Well, the thing is, no one was ever able to

explain how or why they died, and my sense is that Sophia killed them. Oh, she'll give you this whole orphan story, but don't be taken in by her. I know I'm not perfect, I know I'm spoiled rotten, but my heart is always in the right place, and I certainly don't go around being crazy like Sophia does." Audrey seemed irritated as if she needed to justify herself.

She hadn't yet answered my question, though, and I wondered if she was just stalling for time to come up with an answer. "So what about the letter?"

Audrey was unashamedly frank. "She made it up, the whole thing. It's fake. Stefan had no knowledge of her until that day that she walked into his restaurant."

It was a reasonable explanation from what I could see. "But how did she know that you had a job here or where to find you?"

From my close examination of Audrey's face, I felt like she might just be telling the truth, but I wanted to try and keep an open mind.

Audrey continued. "A simple mistake. It was at my graduation ceremony. My tutor Pierre knew that I had got the job here, you see. Stefan had contacted him for a reference when I applied for the job. Well, he was so excited that I, the student with the best grades of the whole cohort, had earned a job at one of the highest award-winning restaurants, that he couldn't help but announce it to all the parents at the presentation ceremony. He must have told everyone about his high-achieving student. Of course, Sophia was at the ceremony too, and people were asking her what her plans were, but she had nothing, no job. She was a failure, and she was jealous of me. Blamed her poor grades on me for breaking her heart and has had a chip on her shoulder ever since. She's always wanted to get revenge somehow, and now here she is trying to cause a rift between me and Stefan, trying to get people to hate me."

I suddenly felt quite sorry for Audrey and wondered if I too had fallen under Sophia's spell and judged Audrey too harshly as a result. I needed to speak with Eloise, get her take on things. "OK. Well, where do we go from here? It's clear that the two of you can't go on like this. It isn't fair on the people around you who feel like they must choose sides. We can't let the rift between you two affect Stefan's restaurant or Emilio's coffee shop."

"I couldn't agree more," Audrey said. "I'd love nothing better than to the bury the hatchet and start afresh, but do you think Sophia would be willing?"

But before I had a chance to speak about

finding a solution, something awful happened. Out of nowhere, the roof of the nook we were in collapsed around us, a long thin shard of ice almost hitting Audrey. If I hadn't pulled her towards me at that very second, it would certainly have pierced her body and killed her outright.

Nicklas came rushing over, moving lumps of ice from around us. "Is everyone OK? Can you hear me?" His voice sounded panicked, and he was very shaken.

I wanted to reassure him so badly, but my voice was shaky.

"Yes, Nicklas, we're OK. It's just myself and Audrey. Part of the roof seems to have collapsed on us." I looked at Audrey, who was in shock and very pale and clammy. "Are you hurt, Audrey?"

It took a moment for her to reply. "I'm OK. I'm OK. Just shaken, I think. I want to go home now. I want Stefan."

Karl did a roll call, the group shaken by the collapse of the small ledge outside the cave. "Nicklas, everyone is present, apart from Sophia, Rose, and Margot."

"I'm here," Sophia said. "Right behind you. What's happened?"

"We're here too," Rose and Margot announced. "Rose needed to spend a penny but didn't want to go on her own, in case she fell down a crevasse, but we're here now."

"Super. Everyone's accounted for, and it seems like no harm was done." Nicklas breathed a massive sigh of relief, but was concerned as to why the roof had collapsed. It just didn't make sense. The structure had been solid enough, and there was no way that the ice could have melted. He pulled Audrey to her feet, and I took his hand too as I dusted myself off.

"Are you guys really alright?" Nicklas looked unconvinced.

I picked up the large icicle that had narrowly missed Audrey. "Yes, Nicklas, really, we're all good." I looked closer at the end of the icicle. It seemed as if it had teeth marks like it had been sawn off rather than broken of its own accord. "Here, Nicklas, what do you think of this? If an icicle broke off, wouldn't you expect it to snap off cleanly? This one looks all crumpled at the edges." I handed it to Nicklas.

"You know what, Madeleine? I think you're right. The collapse looks deliberate to me. I don't think this was an accident at all. But who would want to kill either of you?" I didn't need to answer Nicklas's question. I doubted that anyone here would want to kill me, but pretty much everyone had wanted to kill Audrey at some point or another.

I spotted something on the ground under a piece of the fallen ice. "Oh, has anyone lost a glove? Is it yours, Audrey? I know it's not mine." I looked inside the glove to see if it might have a name in it. Sophia must have read my expression because she snatched it off me quickly.

"Why have you got my glove, Madeleine? Did you steal it? Are you trying to set me up now? I thought you were my friend."

"Now hold on a minute, Sophia. I've just had a near-death experience because someone here tried to kill me, and now you think I'm trying to frame you for it? That's just silly."

Sophia skulked. "Well, explain to me how you have my glove when you know damn well that I lost it in the restaurant and haven't seen it since." Audrey looked at me as confused as I was at Sophia's sudden change of character.

"Told you so," she said. "Sophia's crazy."

I suddenly felt stupid. Had I really been taken in by Sophia? Had she just tried to murder us? I threw the glove at her and walked over to Eloise, passing Violetta in the process.

Eloise did a double-take. "Hang on. I thought you were at the restaurant, Violetta; what are you doing here? I mean, how did you get here? You weren't on the coach?"

Audrey suddenly recovered herself after her near-fatal accident. "Yes, I'd like to know the answer to that too. You're supposed to be looking after the restaurant."

Nicklas stepped in, keen to defend his girlfriend. "Now look here, don't you dare accuse my girlfriend. She's as much right to be here as any of us. It's awful how you treat her, making her do everything for you, and you just swanning off whilst she does all the work. I'm not having it." Nicklas put his arm around Violetta's shoulders as Stefan stepped up to Audrey to comfort her after the cave collapse.

Violetta did not want her boyfriend sticking up for her. "If you must know, the delivery driver came earlier than expected, and because I'd managed to get all the jobs done without you two love birds getting under my feet, I decided to knock off early. There was nothing else left to do. Daan dropped me off on his way to one of the ski runs, and since it was such a nice day, I thought I'd come and join you. Not against the law, is it?"

Eloise could sense that this trek wasn't going to end well if we all stood around arguing, and the first of the tourists would be arriving soon. She needed to get us all back to some sense of normality and fast. "OK, OK, let's just calm things down for a minute. I don't know about you guys, but I'm getting chilly, and we've got guests arriving soon. I think we should start heading back now."

I knew that I would need to back Eloise up. Otherwise, we'd be stuck on the glacier for the rest of the season, bickering with one another. "I agree. I'm sure there are perfectly reasonable explanations for everything. We all just need to calm down. We have a long ski season ahead of us, so let's just try and enjoy it, shall we?"

The rest of the group nodded their heads and picked up their things. The mood was ruined now, and what should have been a fun day had almost ended in disaster. Audrey suddenly let out a scream.

My heart stopped for a moment, wondering what on earth had happened now. Audrey was fumbling around in the ice and looking through her pockets. "My watch. Where is it? I can't find my watch. It was a gift from my father. I was definitely wearing it earlier."

Sophia stood with her hands on her hips, shaking her head. "Yeah, right. Pull the other one. Is this another one of your schemes to blame me for something that I have nothing to do with?"

Audrey did look panicked, and she was

throwing the blocks of ice like crazy. "Not now, Sophia. I've genuinely lost my watch. Why would I lie about something like that? I need to find it. Please, it's important." Audrey was starting to cry again, and nothing would console her.

Sophia refused to move, even after the other group members began to join in the search. "OK. Prove it. Prove that you were wearing a watch. I bet you're just getting us to go on a wild goose chase for your sick amusement."

I was cross with Sophia now. I had seen a very different side of her, and I didn't like it at all. "Don't be silly, Sophia. How can Audrey possibly prove that she has lost her watch?"

"Actually, I think I can prove it," Audrey remarked as she pulled out her iPhone. She flicked through the photos on the screen with a swipe of her finger. "There, you see? I took this photo less than an hour ago at the back of the cave. I'm wearing the same clothes in the photo as I am here, and so is Stefan. You can clearly see the watch on my wrist."

Audrey showed the selfie to everyone in the group. There was certainly no denying it, and to have set up the photos in advanced would have required an awful lot of effort. But it made no difference to the search. The watch was not to be found anywhere, and eventually we had to leave the glacier, defeated in our search.

"Well, that was an eventful excursion." I linked my arm through Eloise's, the events of the day starting to take their toll on me. I felt a little bit homesick suddenly, but was glad to have Eloise here by my side, the only thing I could depend on in life. I relayed my conversation with Audrey to her, Eloise nodding at regular intervals, taking it all in.

"If you'd told me this before Sophia's reaction to Audrey's lost watch, I don't think I would have believed Audrey's version of things at all, but having seen Sophia flip out like that, I'm now starting to wonder." Eloise was processing events as she spoke.

"But if the cave collapse was deliberate, then who do you think could have caused it? I mean, everyone was accounted for, and it couldn't have been me or Audrey because we were the victims, and I don't imagine for a moment that it would be you. Who was with you in the cave when it happened, Eloise?"

Eloise thought long and hard. "Well, if my memory is correct, then everyone was accounted for, apart from Sophia, Rose, Margot, and depending on when Violetta arrived, then her too."

I reflected on our suspects some more. "OK, so if we rule me out as a target and focus on Audrey, then who out of those people has a motive for wanting to kill her? Is there anyone we can eliminate from our enquiry?"

Eloise rubbed her nose. "Violetta seems like a likely suspect to me. She had the motive and the opportunity. We know that she doesn't like working with Audrey at the restaurant, that Audrey treats her as a skivvy, and she could easily have caused the collapse because no one knew that she was even here. She also had access to Sophia's gloves, and could have planted the glove so that suspicion would be cast on Audrey stealing it."

"And what about Rose?" I enquired. "What do we know about her?"

Eloise thought about it for a moment. "We don't know a lot about Rose, but we do know that she is secretary to Audrey's father and that she doesn't want Audrey to sign those legal documents. She certainly had the time and the opportunity to cause the collapse, but we've no idea what the incentive would be for killing Audrey. She seems to have a very neutral relationship with her from what I've seen."

"Right," I added. "Now what about Margot,

Audrey's stepmother? What do we know about her?"

"That's a tricky one." Eloise stopped for a moment to adjust her snow boots. "We know that her name is Margot, she is married to Audrey's father, but she is not Audrey's mother, and there doesn't seem to be much in the way of a relationship between her and Audrey. They seem to get along OK, but I wouldn't say they are close. She does want Audrey to sign the papers, and I don't think she is best pleased that the secretary is here mucking up her plans. She had the opportunity, but what is her motive?"

I knew that we would need a lot more concrete evidence before we could speculate further, and now might be our only chance to get hold of the details. "There's only one thing for it, Eloise: we'll just have to try and gather information from Rose and Margot, get to the bottom of what exactly those papers are and why Rose doesn't want them signed, but Margot does."

"Are you sure you feel well enough for this, Maddy? You have just had a big fright." I was indeed shaken up after getting caught in the collapsed cave, but I knew that the best cure for my nerves was to solve our case. Besides, we worked best as a team, and if we worked together on this, we could get twice the amount of information in half the time. "I'll try and strike up a conversation with Rose, whilst you try and talk with Margot."

I hung back for a moment, letting some of the group walk past me as I pretended to adjust my winter boot and sock. Eloise pretended to wait for me. Rose and Margot were at the back of the group, so we dived in behind them as soon as they passed us, hoping to catch wind of their conversation. But the two ladies didn't speak to each other. We needed to try something else. I signalled to Eloise to go around the side of Rose to strike up a conversation with her, and in time, I would try and speak with Margot.

"Excuse me, ladies," Eloise announced. "Maddy and I were just having an argument about which was better, coffee doughnuts or chocolate doughnuts, and we could use your opinion."

The ladies looked annoyed at being disturbed by two young things, and I had to be careful not to give away my knowledge of French; for now, I wanted to keep that to myself so I could eavesdrop. It was a terrible way to start a conversation, but it was all we could think of on the spot.

Rose was the easier of the two to engage in

conversation, and we managed to find out that she hadn't met Audrey in person before, and that her boss Felix, Audrey's dad, had sent her here on business. It wasn't a lot to go on, but she didn't seem to have any reason for wanting to kill Audrey.

I turned my attention to Margot. "Have you been to Austria before?" I asked.

Margot's face was stern. "We used to come to Austria quite often for skiing holidays, but we don't travel much at all these days, not since..." Margot stopped mid-conversation, realising that she had already said too much. "...since we decided that we're too old to ski anymore. It just doesn't appeal to us these days."

I eyed her inquisitively. "That's a shame. I bet you go on other lovely holidays instead, though, don't you?"

Margot faltered, and I got the impression that she didn't go on holiday anywhere anymore, but it didn't seem to be for lack of wanting to travel as much as she tried to convince me that it no longer interested them. "But you must go to St Tropez surely, what with having the chateau there?"

Margot gritted her teeth. "Chateau? Oh no, we sold that. No one is going to St Tropez these days." This was strange information, given that Audrey had once told me she was going to stay there for the summer. Something didn't quite add up. Something was telling me that Margot was in financial difficulty, and from the sound of it, her relationship with Audrey's father was soon to be over. Out of the two ladies, Margot seemed to have the bigger motive, so that just left her and Violetta as likely suspects.

Chapter 18

Sébastien Paris Pâtisserie, Val D'Isera Ski
Resort, Austria: 1st December 2018

"I really can't believe that we are going for dinner at the Sébastien Paris Pâtisserie. Remind me again how this happened and why we agreed to accept," Eloise said, a large hint of sarcasm in her voice. I was just as surprised as she was.

"Audrey said that she and Stefan wanted to say thank you for saving her life on the glacier, that it was the least they could do. So they have booked us a free dinner at the restaurant for their opening night tonight."

Eloise looked down at her clothes. "I just feel like we're going to be the worst dressed of all the guests. I didn't expect to be dining out at fancy restaurants, so I didn't bring anything to wear."

I looked down at my clothes and agreed. "What I don't get is how Audrey could be so nasty in the cave one moment, and then suddenly full of remorse and saying that Sophia had been harassing her. I mean, I could maybe understand it if she had changed her attitude after nearly getting killed by the icicle, but she didn't; she was like that as soon as we stepped outside. Unless, of course, it was all bravado, and she did genuinely get fed up with trying to be tough."

Eloise was as confused about the whole thing as I was. "The thing is, whichever way you look at it, both sides seem to make sense. If Audrey really was a cow bag to Sophia and really did steal her job from her, then Sophia's behaviour would make sense. But equally, if what Audrey says is true, then it would also explain how sheer exasperation would drive Audrey over the edge."

I knew what we needed to do. "I think we should try and find a letterhead, something that proves or disproves Sophia's letter. It looked genuine enough to me when I saw it, but it could have been faked?"

Eloise wasn't so sure. "I'm not certain that the letter would help us, Maddy. I mean, if Sophia was telling the truth and she did receive it in the post like she says she did, then it still could have been posted to her by Audrey. The stamps on the envelope and postal marks looked genuine enough for it to be real. And even if the branded paper is wrong, we still don't know that Audrey didn't make it look fake on purpose."

Eloise was right. Even if we could get hold of the branded paper from the restaurant, it wouldn't prove things either way. "I just don't understand why Stefan would send the letter by snail mail when he could just as easily have sent it by email? Didn't we both get our job offers by email? Wouldn't it be quicker and cheaper? He doesn't seem like the kind of person that would go to all the effort of going to the post office to buy stamps and to get the letter weighed when he could just reply by email in a fraction of the time, especially as a busy chef."

Eloise thought some more. "Perhaps he isn't very computer savvy?"

I didn't believe this for a second. "He must have a computer, and he must be at least a little computer literate. Sophia said that her interview was done over Skype, and that would explain how she recognised him when she first saw him in the restaurant. But it's weird how he never really acknowledges or speaks to her."

"That's true enough," Eloise remarked. "But

if the Skype interview was a lie from Sophia, then that might explain why he didn't seem to acknowledge her."

I opened the door to the restaurant. It was filled with diners, and everyone looked incredibly well dressed. We were going to stick out like a sore thumb for sure. Stefan rushed over, greeting us with several kisses, alternating cheeks in the way that only French people do, except that Stefan was actually Austrian. But he'd lived in France long enough to pick up the custom, and the guests seemed to like it, so it was good for business, part of the brand. People just assumed that he was French, especially now that he had a fiancée from Paris.

"Welcome, welcome. Please follow me." Stefan shooed away the waiter at the desk and personally led us to a table. It was quite something to see the crystal glasses and many silver utensils on the table. Had we been on a date, it would have been quite romantic in the candlelight. Stefan helped us into our seats and presented us with menus, clicking his fingers at one of the waitresses who now had orders to bring us a bottle of *Château Grand-Puy-Lacoste 2009, Pauillac*.

Eloise kicked me hard under the table as Stefan hurried back into the kitchen. "Have you seen these prices, Maddy? Just look. This wine is listed at 200 euros per bottle, but that's nothing. Some of the wines on this list are in the thousands of euros range. The wine alone must be worth more than all of the cash in the resort ATM."

I had to check the menu for myself. "Well, I hope it tastes nice at that price. We'd better make sure that we drink up every drop."

It was a lovely meal, and the food was superb; that or the wine had gone to our heads. The restaurant was still busy, and we were now on our seventh course as a new bottle of wine appeared at our table. Something sweeter to match our dessert, at Stefan's request, who had chosen the food for us so that we could sample the restaurant's finest. There was no denying that it was a lovely restaurant. No wonder Violetta was always busy cleaning and prepping food for the chefs. Stefan and Audrey must be incredibly busy and stressed out in the kitchen if this was the norm; no wonder they wanted to make the most of any downtime. It made sense for them to pass work on to Violetta during the day when the restaurant was closed.

I somehow couldn't quite picture Sophia working here. She was a great pastry chef for sure, but she did seem to get angry quite easily, and her pastry was nowhere on the same level as these. "You don't suppose Sophia might be lying about

135

getting the highest grades in her year, do you?" I asked Eloise.

"You know, I was just wondering the same thing. These pastries are perfection, and as amazing as Sophia's baking is, I just can't imagine her baking anything on par with these."

I looked at Eloise's cake fork as it cut through the delicate layers of her pastry selection. "I'm also thinking that the chances of both Audrey and Sophia getting the highest grades of the cohort are slim. Surely they couldn't both score the same results?"

Eloise chomped through her pastry. "We need to get in touch with the culinary school, I reckon. Try and get their grades and any references, at least then we will know if either of them is lying."

I tucked into my layered cake slice. "Good thinking. I think we need to speak with Emilio, maybe ask him to contact the school since he's Sophia's boss. But whatever we do, we mustn't let Sophia catch on."

Part Five

Trouble Brewing

Chapter 19

Snow Mountain Café, Val D'Isera Ski Resort, Austria: 2nd December 2018

"Yes, chef," Emilio joked as Sophia ordered him about his kitchen. Sophia threw a cherry at him as Emilio ducked. The coffee shop was already a lot busier, and word had soon gotten around about the cakes and array of coffees on offer. Sophia really had worked her magic at the Snow Mountain Café.

Emilio came out to the counter looking very pleased with himself. "You know, girls, I think you might be my lucky charms. It's only the second day of the ski season, and already the coffee shop has taken more money than it did in the whole of last December. You did me a favour finding

Sophia like that. You'll be in for a payrise if things continue like this."

I didn't want to bring up the subject of Sophia with Emilio yet, not when he was happy with the way things were. I felt a huge burden knowing that we had been responsible for bringing Sophia into his coffee shop. What if she did turn out to be crazy? Who knew what she might be capable of? The implication of what could come sat uneasily in my stomach. But I didn't get a lot of time to ponder on it; we were rushed off our feet and Eloise was throwing order after order at me for different coffees. If I wasn't careful, the whole production line would collapse and the customers would be in an uproar. Thankfully, Eloise and I had several years of Oxford tourists behind us at Mrs Tiggywinkle's and at least here, we could communicate with most of the European tourists between us, with our A-Levels in French and German.

"Here, let's switch over for a bit. I think we could both use a change of scenery." Eloise took my place by the coffee machine, and instead of making up the orders, I rang them up on the till and wrote them down for Eloise instead. It certainly was a nice change, and I soon got back in the flow of things.

"Yes, can I help you?" I repeated for the

thousandth time that day, pretty much on autopilot.

"Oh hey, Maddy. Just a macchiato please." It was Karl, enjoying some downtime after a busy first night at the bar.

"Eat in or take away, Karl?"

"I'll eat in, thanks." Karl glanced around the coffee shop and spotted a table in the corner.

"Great. I'll bring it over when it's ready if you like."

"Um, yeah, that would be awesome. Thanks, Maddy." Karl handed over his euros and I tore off his receipt, placing his order with Eloise. It didn't take her long to get through the backlog, and since there was a small break between customers, I was able to take Karl's drink over to him. Karl was on his mobile by the time I reached his table, and he looked to be deep in conversation, so I put the coffee in front of him and left. I couldn't help but overhear his conversation, and he appeared to be stressed about something.

"Look, I don't know about this, Miryam; it just feels wrong. I mean, what if I get caught? We could both go to prison. OK, OK, I'll try. But I'm not happy about it." Whatever Karl had got himself into, it did not sound good.

As I got back to the counter where Eloise was mopping up the spills from the rush of coffee orders, I ran this latest finding by her. "You don't think Karl could be our suspect, do you? Maybe *he* tried to kill Audrey with the ice collapse because he wanted his brother to have more time with Violetta? We all know that Audrey and Violetta don't much care for each other."

Eloise wrung out the cloth in the sink and turned on the tap to give it a rinse-through. "I don't know. Sure, the brothers are close, but would you risk all that just for your brother's girlfriend?"

"You're right," I added. "It does seem a bit far-fetched. But he's certainly up to something." Karl looked around with a guilty expression on his face as he scooped up his cup and took a sip of the hot coffee. We'd need to keep a closer eye on him, find out what he was up to.

Chapter 20

Snow Mountain Café, Val D'Isera Ski Resort, Austria: 2nd December 2018

"Do either of you want a break now that things have quieted down a little?" Emilio asked. "Sophia says she's happy to work out front for a bit if you want a sit-down."

My feet were aching, even after years of working in Mrs Tiggywinkle's. "Sure, that would be great."

Emilio smiled warmly. "I tell you what, why don't you go and sit down and I'll bring you some drinks and nibbles over. We should be fairly slow for a bit now that folks are on the ski slopes for the afternoon."

I looked around the coffee shop. Things had slowed down compared to the earlier rush, and the orders were far steadier now. Mainly ski widowers, the ones who only came on holiday because they had partners who loved to ski or snowboard. The coffee shop was still full, but the customers were reading books or relaxing and wouldn't be in any hurry to leave. I spotted a couple of seats by Théo and was followed closely behind by Eloise. We were both exhausted after the earlier rush.

Théo patted a hand on the seats near him. "I've been saving these for you," he smiled. "I must say, you have transformed the coffee shop. It's wonderful to see it so busy. Emilio deserves it after all the work he's put in to get the place up and running. It's something very special now."

It was nice of Théo to say that, and I wanted him to know we appreciated his kind words. "Thank you, Théo, but I don't think we can take the credit. Emilio is the one who created a warm and cosy place to sit in and relax, and Sophia is the one who bakes all the yummy cakes. All we do is to supply the punters with coffee as quickly as we can."

"You know, you should take a compliment when it is given," Théo teased. "You really have worked your charm on this place. You should be very proud. Everyone is talking about how wonderful this place is."

"How's the crossword going?" Eloise was keen to steer the conversation to more important matters.

"Not bad at all; in fact. I just finished it when you two arrived." Théo folded up the newspaper and pushed it to one side.

It was time for me to be brave. I needed to ask Théo's advice, but I was worried about how he might react. "I'm sorry to trouble you, Théo, but we badly need to talk to you about a very delicate matter. I hope you don't mind. It's just that we wanted to get your advice as Emilio's friend before we approach him ourselves."

Théo was all ears. "Go on."

Eloise gave me a sideways glance. "I feel a bit stupid now. It sounds silly, but we're worried about Sophia."

Théo leant forward so as not to be heard by any eavesdroppers, Sophia in particular. "Why? Has that girl ... what's her name ... Audrey ... been nasty to her again?"

"On the contrary," I told him. "It seems like it might be Sophia that's being horrid to Audrey, but we've not been able to prove or disprove either side's stories. That's why we need your advice."

"OK," Théo nodded.

"You see, the thing is, you remember that letter that Sophia showed us, with the job offer on it? Sophia says that she received it in the post from Stefan, but Audrey claims that Sophia was never offered the job in the first place, and it would certainly explain why Stefan seems to never acknowledge her. But we can't prove or disprove the letter either way."

I was finding it hard to explain without sounding utterly ridiculous. Eloise helped me out. "Théo, we've no easy way of knowing whether the letter was real or fake, but both Sophia and Audrey told us that they came top in their cohort, and we reckon that *if* we can find out who is telling the truth about *that*, then it would at least give us a starting point for our investigation."

Théo raised an eyebrow. "But what has this got to do with Emilio?"

It was good to talk things through with Théo; if nothing else, it would help us to iron out the flaws in our thinking. "Oh Théo, we feel responsible for Emilio. If Sophia has lied about her qualifications, then it means she really could be as messed up as Audrey says she is, and if that's the case, then she could be dangerous."

Eloise added. "We think she might have tried to kill Audrey up at the glacier the other day, that she intentionally cut down the icicle which caused the cave roof to collapse and the icicle to fall."

Théo inhaled sharply, strumming his fingers on his chin as he thought this through. "Oh, dear. I certainly see your predicament now. But let's imagine that Sophia is, in fact, innocent, and Audrey is the liar. How would that change things?"

I drew in closer to Théo and leant on my elbow. "That's the problem. If we go wading in and Sophia finds out, then if she's guilty, we'll be putting ourselves at risk. If she is innocent, then we'll have lost her trust and respect, and she could truly go off the rails then. That wouldn't be good for Emilio or the café."

Théo picked up the pencil and tapped it on the table. "OK, so basically what we need is for Emilio to contact the culinary school where Audrey and Sophia trained and to ask for their exam results as a prospective employer?"

I nodded at Théo, confirming his suggestion. "But how do we do that without looking like we are trying to find proof and upsetting her?"

"Simple," Théo answered. "We need the culinary school to believe that the two girls are nominees for a local award of some kind, but we need confirmation of their exam results before we can declare the winner."

Eloise sat up straight. "That's genius. Why didn't we think of that, Maddy?"

I wasn't quite sure if we could pull this off alone. "But how do we convince Emilio to contact the culinary school? Won't he know that there is no competition?"

Théo grinned. "Not if *I* happen to be the founder of the competition and enquire myself. I can even set up a baking competition here at the café if it makes things more legitimate."

"Yes, I think that could work," I said as Emilio came over to the fire and joined us for a break.

"You lot look thick as thieves; what are you up to?" Emilio asked with a cheeky grin.

Théo took the lead, saving Eloise and me from telling a fib to our boss. "Emilio, you really have done wonders with the coffee shop, so I was thinking, why not take advantage of the buzz and host a baking competition? I'll even put up the prize fund and be the judge myself; it'll be fun."

Emilio looked delighted. "Oooh, a baking competition! Yes, that would be fun. When can we start?"

"You just leave that to me, Emilio. I could do with a project until my new crossword book arrives. Keep the old brain cells ticking over."

Emilio spat out his coffee. "Old? Théo, you're younger than me. Honestly, you're like a middle-aged man trapped in the body of a youth." Emilio patted his stomach as he laughed a long hard belly laugh.

I was relieved that we had a plan. Théo would contact the culinary school for Audrey and Sophia's grades as part of the competition nomination for best pastry chef, and Emilio would get an actual baking competition at the coffee shop to bring in more customers. Eloise and I would finally find out who was telling the truth and whether Audrey or Sophia had lied to us.

Chapter 21

Sophia Saner, Snow Mountain Café, Val D'Isera Ski Resort, Austria: 2nd December 2018

"Everything OK with you, Sophia? You don't seem your usual cheery self today." Emilio placed a hand gently on the rolling pin that Sophia had been using to flatten out the pastry.

Sophia gave him no eye contact as she huffed and tutted. "I'm fine."

Emilio laughed. "Sure, you just like to murder the pastry for no good reason at all. I thought you said you needed to caress pastry?" Emilio switched the weight to his other hip and folded his arms as he raised a sceptical eyebrow.

Sophia slammed the rolling pin down on the

bench and looked up at him. "OK, so I'm *not* fine. But do you *blame* me? How would you feel if everyone in the resort was accusing you of attempted murder? I wasn't anywhere near the ice cave when the roof collapsed and the icicle fell, and I've *no* idea how my glove came to be there. Why won't anyone believe me?" Sophia started to cry.

Emilio walked up to her and hugged her. "There, there. The truth will always come out in the end, and the tourists will soon fly back home and be replaced with new ones. What's most important is that I believe you, and so do your friends. It doesn't matter what anyone else thinks."

A sulking Sophia sobbed hard. "It's alright for you. You've got your coffee shop, and Stefan has his restaurant, and the rest of you have got everything all figured out. But what about me? I mean, I've got no one, no family, no money, no long-term prospects. What happens when the ski season is over? No one will ever employ me when they see that my only jobs have been as a pot washer. Don't get me wrong, I'm incredibly grateful to you for the work and letting me bake, but if I'm going to become a professional pastry chef, then I need to be working at restaurants with awards and stars."

"No offence was taken at all, Sophia. I completely understand. It just goes to show how passionate you are about your profession. I admire that in you. It only makes me prouder to have been a part of your journey. Things might seem bleak now, but you'll move forward. You'll achieve your dreams if you continue to work hard, I promise you."

Sophia nodded through heavy tears.

"Come now, Sophia. I've sent the girls to have a break. Why don't you dry your eyes? If you can cover the front for half an hour or so, then we'll spend the afternoon in my treasure trove looking for rare beans and ingredients for your next concoction. What do you think about that?"

"OK." Sophia nodded, cheering up a little.

Chapter 22

Ski Shop, Val D'Isera Ski Resort, Austria: 3rd December 2018

Daan placed the ski boot on the counter and dug around inside the liner with his hand, feeling for a loose edge.

"Hmm, I can't feel any rough edges. What about your sock; how does that feel?"

The lady bent down and pulled off her tubular ski sock, revealing brightly painted toenails. She slipped her arm into the sock and felt around for the source of the sharp, scratchy feel. "Ahaha. Yes, Daan, I think you are right." She pulled a thorn from her sock and slipped it back on her foot. "Problem solved."

Daan smiled. "I know my ski boots, Mrs Vicini."

"Please, call me Camilla," Mrs Vicini encouraged him. "Mrs Vicini makes me feel old."

Her daughter grimaced. "You are old, Mother."

Mrs Vicini looked wildly at her daughter, rather irritated by her offspring. "Oh, hush now, Francesca. Stop being such a whiny teen. It doesn't suit you."

Her daughter stormed off. "Whatever, Mother!"

"Sorry about that, Daan. Honestly, teenagers these days. You'd think they'd be delighted that you'd taken them off skiing for the holidays. She'd have been far happier if I'd simply left her at home, locked in her bedroom with access to the internet.

Daan nodded politely. It was best not to get involved in family arguments, and he certainly saw all sorts of families here in the ski shop. It had been a very busy morning.

"Ahh mate, am I glad to see you!" Daan hugged Karl as he handed him a cup of coffee from the coffee shop. "Courtesy of Maddy and Eloise. They thought you might need it, dude."

Daan took a long sip and smacked his lips together. "Hot, strong, and black; just how I like it.

Those girls really do know how to make a decent cup of coffee. Honestly, I thought I might start to lose my patience with some of the customers today. It's always the same. The first days they start excited and happy, by midholiday they are getting bored, and by the end of the week, they've all fallen out and can't wait to get back home. You couldn't write this stuff, I tell you." Daan took another long drink of his coffee. "How's Nicklas after the glacier incident?"

Karl shook his head. "Hard to tell. He acts like it was just one of those things, but it's doing his head in."

Daan tutted. "Poor bloke. Still, at least no one was hurt."

Karl looked hesitant.

"What?" asked Daan, curious at seeing the expression on Karl's face. "What is it, buddy?"

Karl sucked in the air. "I dunno. I probably should just keep my mouth shut, but, well … I kind of think that maybe it will do him good in some way. You know, to have things go wrong for once. He's always been so perfect; he's always been the favourite son."

Daan laughed. "What do mean 'favourite son?' You're twins, for God's sake; how can your parents possibly have favourites?"

Karl's face dropped into a frown. "But that's

the thing. We might be twins, but we're not identical, and they were only expecting the one baby. They had no idea I was there too. I always feel like I'm intruding on their relationship with their favourite son somehow. Nicklas is the one they wanted; I was just the spare, the backup brother. And why wouldn't they be proud of him? He's one of the youngest people to qualify as a mountain guide, and he's already been selected to join the Swedish snowboard team trials for the next winter Olympics. What have I got to offer them? I'm a bartender and not a very good one at that."

Daan shook his head. "I think you're overreacting, mate. You're probably just tired. What time did you finish up at the bar last night?"

Karl shrugged his shoulders. "I dunno. Maybe 4 am by the time everyone had left and I'd cleaned up all the glasses."

"And what time is it now? I'll tell you what time it is: 8 am, Karl, which means you've not had enough sleep. You'll feel loads better once you've had a kip and got your mojo back or whatever it is you seem to have lost."

"I know, I know. You're probably right," Karl answered

Daan laughed. "What do you mean, 'probably

right?' Of course, I'm right. Now get out of here and go get some shut-eye."

Karl high-fived Daan. "Thanks, dude. I appreciate the pep talk." Karl turned to leave, suddenly remembering why he'd come to the ski shop in the first place. "Oh yeah, I forgot. I came for some of those new sunglasses you got in. Can I have a look?"

Daan was gobsmacked. "Are you for real? You do know how much they cost, right? Those bar shifts must be paying you well."

"What?" Karl looked guilty but quickly relaxed his shoulders, realising he looked suspicious. "Haha. Nice one. No, I promise I've not robbed a bank or anything. Been saving up. Not like I've got anything else to spend my money on, is it?"

Daan took the key out of his pocket for the glass display cabinet. "Hey, I was only joking, mate; it's your money. Good on you, I say. Why shouldn't you treat yourself? You've worked hard for it, dude."

Chapter 23

Snow Mountain Café, Val D'Isera Ski Resort, Austria: 3rd December 2018

Margot came to a standstill outside the coffee shop as she fumbled around in her handbag for her mobile phone. It was ringing loudly, playing a very dramatic tune. She looked around the street rather embarrassed.

"Hello, my *darling* Felix" she answered sarcastically. "Audrey? No, she's not with me right now. I'm just in the town picking up a few things. *No*, I *haven't* signed the divorce papers yet. Look, Felix, I know your little tricks. You're the one who had the affair with your secretary, not me. I don't see why I should suffer because of your infidelity. And that daughter of yours is no better. She's using this Stefan. He's as much as admitted it to me himself. Look, I'm not speaking to you when you're in a mood like this. You can call me later once your manners are restored. Goodbye."

Margot tapped the red button on the screen, hanging up on her husband. She looked hot and bothered as she glanced around, hoping that no one had heard her lose her temper with her soon-to-be ex. Not even Audrey knew about their divorce plans yet, and as much as she couldn't stand the girl, she'd prefer that Audrey heard the news from her and not some stranger.

Margot's phone rang out loudly again. Margot muttered under her breath as she lifted the phone to her ear.

"I've just told you, Felix. I'm *not* interested in anything you've got to say to me right now. Phone me back when … hello? Hello? Who is this? How did you get this number?" Margot steadied herself against a shop window. The caller was not her husband. "Look, OK. I'll get you the money soon. What? I *know* I already said I'd pay you and I haven't. But things have been … well … *complicated*. I'm working on it. You'll have the money soon. No! That's ridiculous. What do you mean the money has doubled? Now you listen to me — "

Margot fell silent as a man walked past her on the snow-covered pavement, recognising him from the coffee shop. But she was certain there was no way he had been able to overhear her conversation. Margot lowered her voice to speak, but the caller had hung up, the subject not on the table for discussion.

Margot was shaking, and she quickly stuffed her phone back into her handbag. She needed a drink to calm her nerves. She unintentionally followed the man who had passed her in the street, and he smiled as he opened the door of the coffee shop for her.

"You see, who says the art of chivalry is dead?" The man waved her in before him, tipping his woolly hat as he opened the door to the welcome sight of his friend Emilio. Margot hurried in, keen not to draw unnecessary attention to herself right now.

"How come you never tip your hat or open doors for me like that, Théo?" Emilio joked.

Théo laughed loudly. "Because, my dear friend, you are not half as beautiful as this lady. That, and you smell like coffee beans, not Parisian perfume."

Margot scurried to the counter without saying a word. She was not in the mood for jokers. Théo and Emilio glanced at each other as Emilio quietly told Théo that the lady hadn't appreciated his charm.

Emilio made his way to the counter, calling out to Théo as he walked. "The usual, Théo?"

Théo gave a pretend bow as he made for his favourite seat. "That, my good sir, would be delightful."

"GOOD MORNING," I said as Margot stood at the counter in front of me. "What can I get you?"

Margot looked even sourer today, despite my best efforts to provide a friendly service. "What? Oh, I'll have a large decaf black coffee. And make sure it's hot, will you? None of this lukewarm muck."

I was surprised at how rude she was, but I continued to be polite all the same. "Certainly, Madame. I'll bring it over to you. Where are you sitting?"

Margot snapped. "Sitting? Sitting? Young lady, I've barely had a chance to get in the door, let alone find a seat to sit in. Zut alors!"

"Excuse me?" I said, thinking I had misheard.

Margot gave me a look that could kill. "What? Look, just get me the damned coffee, will you. How much is it? You know what, just bring it over to me." Margot slammed some coins on the counter as Emilio shrugged his shoulders at me, pulling a comical face to ease my interaction with the crabby woman.

"Blame Théo," Emilio laughed under his breath once Margot had gone to find her seat. I looked at Théo, who was finding the situation funny. I raised my fist at him in jest, knowing that he was sure to supply me with the full details later.

I carried the coffee over to the table where Margot was sitting and nervously placed it in front of her.

"I'm sorry," she apologised. "Bad day. I've just had some awful news, that's all, and it rather knocked me for six."

I smiled kindly, happy that she had seen that her behaviour was not very nice. "Don't worry about it; we've all been there. I'm sure it will come right in the end, whatever it is. Enjoy your coffee."

I was about to return to the counter, but Théo waved me over. "What was all that about?" he inquired.

"I've no idea. I was rather hoping that you could tell me. After all, Emilio did say that you started it," I whispered to Théo, careful not to look too suspicious.

Théo pretended to ask me some crossword

questions, and I mimed as if I was looking at the newspaper questions. "I think the bad mood began long before I opened the door for her, if you know what I mean." Théo tapped the side of his nose. He was being silly as always, trying to make light of the situation. "I heard her on the telephone. It sounded like someone was giving her grief, as she owed them a lot of money. She said the papers hadn't been signed yet, that things were not going to plan, but she was working on it. Does that mean anything to you, Maddy?"

It made complete sense to me, but I needed more evidence before I could tell anyone. "Actually, Théo, I think it does. I have a theory anyway."

Part Six

Queen of Doughnuts

Chapter 24

Snow Mountain Café, Val D'Isera Ski Resort, Austria: 4th December 2018

I wasn't a bad baker before I arrived at the Snow Mountain Café, but after all of Sophia's baking lessons and tips and tricks, I was getting rather good. Doughnuts were now my speciality, and with Sophia's help, I had started to get a bit of a reputation amongst the resort staff and tourists as 'Madeleine, Queen of the Doughnuts.' Emilio was happy too, since there was now a regular queue of people waiting for the Snow Mountain Café to open before they hit the slopes for a day of skiing. Owing to the demand for doughnuts, I had started to come in earlier so that I'd have the chance to bake enough cakes before the coffee shop opened each day.

I'd gotten into quite a nice routine already, even though it was only my first week, but I'd spent a little time on the slopes skiing before letting myself into the café. Emilio had been kind enough to get keys cut for Eloise and me so that we would be able to open and close, freeing him up for other activities, like snowboarding and teaching yoga to the skiers.

Today I decided to have a go at red velvet doughnuts but with a bit of a twist — Sophia's idea — I'd add some winter spices to them, like nutmeg and cinnamon.

It was a bit nippy when I arrived at the coffee shop, and I wasn't naturally a morning person. If I'd been out on the slopes for a quick ski with Daan or for a run in the snow with Nicklas, then I was usually warm and awake enough to begin my day. But this morning, I had been tired and was a bit chilled, having not got the blood pumping. I had to light the fire when I arrived and switched on the water boiler, ready to make my first coffee. I pressed play on the stereo and danced around to get my body going. I laughed at myself because I seemed to have become a baking Olympian, and this was my warm-up routine before the intense session began.

I reached up to a shelf and pulled down a mug for my coffee, which was now percolating through the filter, and spooned in a little sugar and some milk. The smell of the beans alone was enough to send my senses roaring. Reaching for some powdered chocolate to go on top of the milky froth, I spotted a note pinned to the counter:

Hey, Maddy, hope you have a brill morning of baking little mouthfuls of art. A couple of the chalets called me late last night to ask for some of your breakfast doughnuts. Can you bake around 50 of those if you can spare the time? Seems they are proving to be very popular indeed! Have a fab day. Loads of love, Emilio x

P.S. I'm dying to try your red velvet doughnuts. They sound A-M-A-Z-I-N-G!!

"Awww thanks, Emilio," I said out loud to myself, smiling inwardly. I still couldn't believe how lucky I was to be working here, not just with my best friend Eloise, who was still fast asleep at the chalet, but with some of the loveliest people I could have wished for. Working with Sophia in the kitchen was incredible, and Emilio was kind to us and gave us loads of freedom to be creative.

I took a long sip of my coffee. "Phhh!" I'd forgotten how hot my coffee would be, and I burnt my tongue as I took a large slurp, fanning my mouth as the boiling liquid went down my throat and spilt down my top. "You really are an idiot sometimes, Madeleine Cooke." I gasped out loud, laughing at how ridiculous I could be at times. Of course, the coffee was going to be hot; I'd just made, it for goodness sake! I mopped up my coffee spills and felt my tongue against the back of my teeth. It was going to be numb for the rest of the day now, making it difficult to taste things properly. I'd be chopping my fingers off whilst I baked or having accidents if I didn't get my act together.

I carried my mug into the kitchen and switched all the lights on in the hopes that the lighting might help me to feel a bit more awake and washed my hands in the sink before wiping down my baking table. Sophia had left me the recipe and a little sticky note.

Here's the recipe for you as promised, have
fun xx

I looked down the list as I held the paper in

my hand. Flour, sugar, red food colour, oil ... it looked straightforward enough. I took the paper with me and stretched out my arms and back as I walked into the pantry. I felt very humbled to have access to Emilio's secret baking pantry, and a little like a mad scientist or a witch as I scoured the rows of glass jars for my unique and rare ingredients. I longed to try all the coffee and cocoa beans from Emilio's travels, along with the spices, powders, and seeds that I didn't recognise. I was only grateful that Emilio was obsessed with labelling all the jars. Otherwise, I wouldn't have known one bean from the next. Some things just looked the same to me.

I ran my finger along the shelf, searching for the jars labelled with an N. Emilio was a stickler for everything being stored in alphabetical order, and woe betide anyone who didn't put things back in their correct place. These jars were Emilio's babies, each having travelled hundreds of miles to reach their little place on his special shelves.

"Got ya." I grabbed the jar of nutmeg that Emilio had sourced from the island of Grenada in the West Indies and took out one of the round balls. It had already been used before, so it was partially ground down on one side. "Right. Now to find the cinnamon and other spices."

There, I had everything I needed. Time to

begin my baking. I just hoped that my recipe would work.

Chapter 25

Sébastien Paris Pâtisserie, Val D'Isera Ski
Resort, Austria: 4th December 2018

"What exactly do you call that? How am
I supposed to cook? Honestly,
Violetta, it's like you don't care about
this restaurant. If you're not interested, I suggest
you get a job somewhere else." Audrey scraped
Violetta's chopped fruit into the pedal bin,
dropping the lid down on it with a large bang.

"You do know that was the last of the fresh
pineapple, right?" Violetta said.

Audrey's face turned a deep shade of crimson.
"What?"

Violetta opened her mouth to repeat what she
had said, but Audrey stopped her. "I heard you

the first time, you silly girl. What I don't understand is why you would waste all these beautiful, quality ingredients with sloppy chopping? It's like you deliberately want the restaurant to close. Stefan and I are working our butts off here to make something of ourselves, and you just seem to be continually sabotaging us."

Audrey threw the chopping board into the sink. "I'll have to tell Stefan that there's a menu change now. I honestly don't think you appreciate how much time and effort goes into creating a restaurant of this calibre. Every wine must be hand-picked and specially ordered as the perfect accompaniment for each dish. And each course is chosen because it balances the course precisely. Now you've completely *ruined* everything."

The usually placid Violetta finally cracked as Audrey pushed her too far. She took off her apron and threw it at Audrey. "I'm going for a cigarette."

Audrey ran her fingers through her hair impatiently and screamed in frustration.

"Everything OK, my love?" Stefan crept up behind Audrey and put his hands around her waist, kissing her on the neck.

"No, everything is not OK. It's far from OK. I just don't understand what is wrong with these people! It's sickening enough that they want to murder me, but now they want to ruin the restaurant too. That Violetta simply must go. She's no interest in being here whatsoever."

"Aww, come on now, Audrey, I'm sure it's not that bad. Look, why don't you go and take a break for a bit? I'll fix things here."

"Are you sure, babe? There's so much to do still, and we're fully booked tonight." Audrey sighed with relief. "I don't know how I'd cope without you. Everything's just getting on top of me now, between Rose and Margot and those wretched inheritance papers, and Sophia trying to murder me. Seriously, I've had enough of everything. I don't know how much more I can take of this."

"Shush, babe. Go on. I'll sort things out with Violetta." Stefan kissed Audrey and pointed her towards the kitchen door.

STEFAN PULLED some paper from a notepad and started to make a list of jobs for Violetta. One way or another he needed to make things right for the sake of the restaurant. He picked up a doughnut and went out the back. Violetta was on the phone, no doubt to her boyfriend Nicklas, but she hung up as soon as she saw Stefan and put out her cigarette on the ground beneath her foot.

Stefan gave her a little smile. I hear Audrey's giving you a hard time. She's just worried, that's all. Here, I thought you might need a sugar boost." Stefan handed Violetta the doughnut. It was still hot, and she had to blow on it before she could eat it.

"Thanks, Stefan. You're a star."

"No worries. Listen, I've drawn up a list of things we still need to do before we open tonight. Can you do me a huge favour and get them done while I'm out? I need to go and see someone for a bit. Have a break first though, and feel free to put some music on as you work. Audrey won't be back any time soon, so you'll have the kitchen to yourself.

"Sure thing, Stefan. You know I'd do anything for you. Look, I'm sorry about earlier, I didn't mean to snap; believe it or not, I would quite like to keep my job here."

Stefan shook his head. "Seriously, don't sweat it. Audrey has that effect on people. She's a driven chef; they get like that sometimes, we all do. It comes with the territory."

Chapter 26

Ski Shop, Val D'Isera Ski Resort, Austria: 4th December 2018

"Can I help you, Madame?" Daan asked as a rather on edge Margot Baillieu-Flandin hid behind a clothing rail in the ski shop. There was no one else around, so he was flummoxed by what, or who, exactly she might be hiding from. But he had seen her here quite a lot of late, and she never bought or hired any ski gear on her visits.

Several tourists had complained that they had lost watches here in the shop whilst trying on ski gear, and Daan was starting to suspect that Audrey's stepmother Margot might have something to do with it. Daan had been so worried that he'd spoken to Stefan and Audrey directly. The last thing that Daan wanted was to get the frumpy-looking lady into trouble with the Austrian police, but he was starting to wonder if she might be suffering from one of those mental health conditions where ladies of a certain age (and often so wealthy that they needed for nothing), steal stuff just to see if they could get away with it, or because it is their way of crying out for help. Kleptomania, Stefan had called it when he consulted with him about his mother-in-law to-be. The problem was, if Margot was stealing the watches, then she wasn't making it easy for him to catch her in the act.

Daan hesitated for a moment, wondering what to do. But he had promised to call Audrey and Stefan the moment he found her acting suspiciously in the ski shop.

Daan pulled out his phone and dialled the number, but when he looked up again at the rails, Margot had gone.

IT WAS FRIGHTFULLY COLD OUTSIDE. An icy wind blew fresh powdery snow into the eyes of the few people who were already out and about on the streets of Val D'Isera. Which was few, since most of the tourists were sitting at breakfast tables in their toasty warm chalets, stuffing their faces with food served to them by their chalet maids. The only people up early enough to pace the streets at this hour were the locals and the odd staff member, enjoying the solitude of a resort without guests demanding constant attention.

Margot pulled her scarf up around her neck as a drip fell from her very red nose. She desperately needed to make this phone call, but it was proving to be difficult finding a place where no one else might hear her. She couldn't do it at Audrey's place with Audrey and Stefan hanging around, nor could she go to the coffee shop because it wasn't open yet. If it weren't for the biting wind, she might have made the call from the street in the deserted town centre, but right now her fingers were frozen solid, and the touch screen on her phone had stopped responding in the low temperature.

Spotting a light in the ski shop, and knowing that the guy who worked there, Daan, liked to open early in case any skiers wanted to set out for the higher ski runs, Margot decided that the ski shop would be the best location to make her call from.

Margot pushed the door gently, trying to minimise the sound of it opening. She could see the young man, Daan, outback sorting ski gear for Nicklas's clients, and he had the Val D'Isera radio station playing on his laptop. Chances were he wouldn't even notice she was here.

Margot crouched down as low as she could and scurried across to one of the large racks of new ski gear, ducking down so that Daan wouldn't see her. She peered around the side of the rail and, as predicted, Daan was busy looking at his phone.

She pulled out her phone just as the caller's number flashed on the screen. She had wanted to call the number herself, but the caller had beaten her to it. Not a good position to be in.

Margot spoke into the phone. "I was just about to call you. I'll have the money, OK, just give me a little more time. I'll meet you at the Snow Mountain Café in a bit. Everything is in place, as we discussed."

Chapter 27

Snow Mountain Café, Val D'Isera Ski Resort, Austria: 4th December 2018

The cold, grey days at the coffee shop were already my favourites, and it seemed as if the whole of the Val D'Isera Ski Resort agreed with me. We were rushed off our feet all morning, and it was all Eloise and I could do to keep up with the coffee and hot chocolate orders. We were running out of everything fast, and I wished I'd had more time to bake things to sell.

I was about to put the red velvet doughnuts out on display, but Eloise took the plate from me and put them back on the kitchen table. "Sophia suggested that we'd best keep those until the afternoon, Maddy. Otherwise, we'll have nothing left to sell, and you know how cranky customers get when their sugar levels get low!"

"Good idea." I agreed as I looked around at the people sitting enjoying the warmth, music, and mixed scent of coffee, cakes, and hot chocolate. We were packed. Some customers were even leaning against walls, waiting for tables to become available. It reminded me of Mrs Tiggywinkle's back in Oxford, and I found myself wishing Mrs B were here to see Eloise and I now that we were out in the world, learning all these skills. My French had improved no end, and Eloise's German was getting a lot of practice too. We were a great team, especially now that Sophia had been teaching us about baking. "You must *never*, ever lick the bowl or eat the cake mixture," Sophia had told me quite sternly. She was usually kind and gentle, but when it came to her pastries, she could be quite a force to be reckoned with. "It's incredibly unprofessional." She was right, of course; it wasn't brilliant from a hygiene perspective and I should have known better, but the temptation to clean up a bowl that was finished with had been too great.

Margot entered the coffee shop, and I noticed that she looked just as miserable today as she had the other day. Thankfully, we seemed to have come to an unspoken truce.

I was expecting her to be a little more civil after her last visit, but I hadn't expected her to greet me by name and so politely, and it took me aback for a moment. "Good morning, Miss Madeleine. A cup of strong black coffee, no milk or sugar, to stay, if you please." Eloise gave me an odd glance, opening her eyes wide as if in shock.

"Certainly. One strong black coffee coming up. If you are quick, I think I just saw a seat become available over there. If you go grab it, I'll bring your coffee to you.

Eloise put her hands out in front of her, palms up, her way of expressing her surprise at what had just happened. "Look at you, all best buddies with Margot Baillieu-Flandin. Tell me I just entered a parallel universe. What did you do to her? Poison her doughnuts?"

"What? God, no! Eloise, don't be saying I've poisoned the doughnuts; you know how fast news spreads in this place." I was half-joking, but still, it wasn't the kind of thing that should be said so loud and openly, even in jest.

An Italian lady, Camilla Vicini, and her daughter Francesca were in the queue waiting to be served. Camilla threw me a proper death stare as if I might have poisoned the doughnuts. I hurriedly defended myself. "Don't mind her, that's just my best friend Eloise, and it was a *joke*. I wouldn't poison the doughnuts, not ever. Cross my heart and hope to, well, you know … die." Camilla had been just about to order one of my orange blossom doughnuts from the counter, but changed her mind at the last moment and instead pointed to a slice of Battenberg cake. There was no point trying to convince her otherwise; it would only make things worse.

Francesca had her headphones on and didn't realise how loudly she was speaking. "I bloody would. Have you met half the people around here? Seriously, they are all so dumb and complaining all the time. I don't know how you guys put up with them."

Camilla looked furious as she shouted at her daughter, "Francesca, that's enough! Honestly, I don't know what's gotten into you these days!" Camilla leant in close to her daughter, pushed back the headphones from one ear, and quietly asked her a very personal question, which only made Francesca madder. "Have you got your period? Is that it? Because if it is, I'll understand completely. It would certainly explain why you are so cranky all the time."

Camilla was trying to be helpful but her motherly instinct was a bit out of kilter. Francesca flushed bright red and stormed off. "For flip's sake, Mother. Talk about embarrassing. I hate you."

Camilla stood alone at the counter, confused as to why her daughter had said that she hated her. I felt quite bad for them both. They were close but struggled to communicate how they felt about each other.

A flustered Camilla placed her order and paid by card as Eloise placed her coffee and cakes at the end of the counter. "She'll grow out of it; I really wouldn't worry. I'm sure our mothers despaired of us too, eh Maddy?" I nodded, though I didn't believe for a moment that either of us was as much of a handful as Francesca seemed to be. But to be fair, Eloise and I had both decided to leave home so that we could board at the school and focus on building up our future detective agency. We had probably managed to avoid a lot of that whole weird parent-teen relationship, and our parents had treated us like grown-ups since day one, expecting us to become lawyers or some other respectable professional. We'd never actually admitted to them that we were going to open our detective agency one day.

There was a slight lull in the queue, and Eloise suggested that we make the most of the opportunity and clear some of the cups and plates from the tables before the backlog of crockery to be washed became out of hand.

Eloise was an expert in table clearing, and after all our years working in Mrs Tiggywinkle's coffee shop, we had developed a system that allowed us to work very efficiently as a team.

"I'll start over there, and you start there, and we'll meet in the middle. Any customers come in, you go serve them, and I'll continue clearing," Eloise remarked.

I grabbed two cloths from the sink and flicked one into Eloise's hand. "Got it. Race you?"

Eloise looked me dead in the eye, her evil grin apparent as it always was when we got competitive. "Ready, steady, *go!*"

Poor Sophia didn't know what had hit her as she found herself surrounded by the two of us armed with cups and saucers and plates and cutlery. She didn't look very impressed, but there was little we could do about it. There was no opportunity to clear tables when we had long queues, and we needed to have one of us on the till and the other making the drinks and serving the cakes. Customers just didn't come in nice, steady flows; they arrived in chaotic bursts, and the only time we had to clear tables was when there were gaps in the queue. It was tough luck; Sophia would just have to get over it.

Eloise rubbed her hands together. "There. That looks loads better."

I smiled at a job well done as I noticed Stefan walking across the coffee shop towards the counter. It was unusual to see him in here; he was usually too busy preparing for the evening guests at the restaurant, but he looked to be on business, wearing a fancy suit and carrying a briefcase. Very official. He spotted Margot in the corner and gave her a little wave, but she didn't look overly pleased to see him. I got the impression that their relationship was strained. He placed his order with Eloise at the till, and I made his drink. He seemed quiet and serious today, not quite his usual self like he was somehow preoccupied, so we left him to it, and he spent most of his visit on the phone.

Sophia came out to the counter for a few moments. It was clear that she no longer trusted us to clear the tables efficiently, and she doubted us when we said that we hadn't intentionally brought everything out to her at once. We knew that she had come out to check that we were clearing tables as and when we could.

"It doesn't look *that* busy," Sophia observed, unaware that this was not how the coffee shop had looked moments ago when a coach load of people arrived off one of Nicklas' glacier tours. "Why don't you try and clear the tables as soon as the customer is done?" Sophia advised as if we were new to barista work.

I was a bit annoyed at Sophia's attitude, to be honest. Eloise and I had worked hard all morning and felt that we couldn't have done any more. Besides, Emilio was very happy, and if anyone was to criticise, it should have been him as our employer, not Sophia, who wouldn't even have the job if it weren't for Eloise and I asking Emilio to hire her.

Eloise was annoyed too. "Because Emilio doesn't like it when staff hover over the customer's shoulders waiting for them to finish eating. He wants them to feel at home, and I completely agree. It's a coffee shop, not a fast food restaurant."

Sophia huffed. "Fine. I'll just have to clear the tables myself."

I didn't want to tell tales on Sophia, but she was out of order, especially criticising us like that in front of customers. Luckily, the customer who heard what she said was Théo. He wasn't impressed either. "That was bang out of order. She should *not* be speaking to you like that or undermining Emilio. I think I'll have a word with him if that's OK with you. You do a great job, Emilio's always saying so."

Eloise was cross. "You know, I'm starting to

believe that we don't know Sophia as well as we first thought. One minute she's nice as pie, the next she completely flips. Maybe Audrey was right about her after all. Did you hear anything back from the culinary school yet, Théo?" I'd seldom seen Eloise ruffled like she was, in all our years as friends. Sophia had gotten to her.

Théo shook his head. "Sadly not. They're closed for a public holiday but said they would call me in a few days. I should hear something very soon."

Emilio had been absent for most of the morning, meeting with the bank manager, but he probably would have wished that he hadn't returned to the coffee shop at the exact moment that he did. Camilla spotted him from across the room and came over to say hello in a rather affectionate way.

Théo started laughing. "I think Emilio has a lady friend; look over there."

Eloise and I laughed too, Théo was right, there seemed to be some chemistry between them.

Meanwhile, her daughter Francesca was sitting at the table, her arms crossed and headphones on, but her mother looked very pleased to see Emilio. Sophia was moving plates and cups around Francesca and removed

191

Camilla's half-drunk cup of coffee, even though it was clear that she had only left it to go and say hello to Emilio. Francesca was trying hard to get the cup off Sophia, but Sophia would not relinquish it "But my mother hasn't finished drinking it yet." Francesca protested, to no avail.

Sophia snatched the cup of coffee from Francesca's hand and was met by protests from a couple of the customers who had seen what had happened, one of whom was Stefan. He was trying hard to calm her, but it was only making her more annoyed. "Sophia, isn't it? Look, I'm sure Emilio won't mind if you leave this cup of coffee here with the girl. It isn't a big deal. No need to behave so irrationally over it. It's *just* a cup."

Sophia suddenly lost her temper. "*Just* a cup! *Just* a cup! How *dare* you. If it wasn't for you, I'd be a top pastry chef by now instead of washing up pots and pans in the back and working with these imbeciles."

Stefan placed a hand on her arm, trying to calm her down. But it only made matters worse. "*Get* your hands *off* me, you disgusting old man. Who exactly do you think you are? Don't touch me!"

The argument escalated, Sophia's protestations incoherent and nonsensical as the customers watched on in horror. Without warning, Sophia threw the cup of coffee over Stefan along with a bottle of water that was on the table.

Stefan stood up in surprise, accidentally knocking the table flying as the coffee ran down his face and all over his smart business suit. Sophia flinched and pulled away, raising her arms in protest. "I'm … I'm … I'm so sorry. Please …. forgive me …. I didn't mean it … I just don't know what came over me." Sophia collapsed to the floor and began to sob. Emilio was too much in shock to move, or he probably would have come over and thrown Sophia out of the coffee shop at that very moment. How had he been such a bad judge of character? Had he been swayed by her qualifications and gone against his better judgement?

Emilio finally pulled himself together and came over to where the commotion had happened. "Sophia, come outside with me, please. Let's go and get some fresh air, shall we? Stefan, I am *so* sorry. I've never known anything like this to happen in my coffee shop before." Emilio tried to lead Sophia away, but she began shouting and protesting her innocence and asking forgiveness again.

Théo presented Stefan with a selection of

napkins so he could at least wipe the coffee from his face and arms.

But to everyone's surprise, Stefan was calm and forgiving. "Please … really … it's no big deal … honestly … look, it's coming off already … I'll just nip into the bathroom and wash the coffee off my shirt and it'll be good as new in no time. There's no need to punish her; she's distressed. We've all had days like that. Please don't do anything on my account. And whatever happens, you mustn't let Audrey find out. Things are bad enough between her and Sophia as it is without this as well." Stefan picked up his case and headed to the coffee shop's toilet as Margot opened the toilet door and stepped out of the cubicle, acknowledging him as she passed. She didn't seem to even notice that he was covered in coffee or that the coffee shop had gone silent in the wake of Sophia's outburst. Margot was in a world of her own.

Eventually, Emilio and Théo managed to drag Sophia into the back and sat her down at the kitchen table with a drink. Emilio didn't know what to do; it wasn't something he'd ever had to deal with before.

"Look, Sophia, I think it's probably best that you go home for now and take a few days off, then we'll decide what to do next. I obviously can't have my staff treating customers like that, but equally, you seem like a nice enough person, and your behaviour today seems very out of character. I can't say fairer than that right now. I'm still too much in shock."

STEFAN CAME out of the toilet, having washed his top in the sink and dried it under the hand drier for several minutes. It didn't look too bad, all things considered. He clutched his bag under his arm and stepped back out into the coffee shop where everyone had gone back to their conversations now that all the drama was over.

Emilio came rushing over to Stefan with a large paper bag in his hand. He passed the bag to Stefan. "Call it a peace offering. Red velvet doughnuts, Madeleine made them this morning. Secret recipe. I'm more than happy to pay for the dry cleaning too; just send me the bill."

Stefan took the bag of doughnuts with gratitude and assured Stefan he wouldn't be placing charges or lodging any complaints. "What I'd really like, Emilio —"

Emilio nodded his head quickly. "Anything, anything at all …. "

Stefan rolled the top of the paper bag down,

sealing the doughnuts in. "What I'd like is for Sophia to get some help and support for whatever is going on with her, and please promise me she won't lose her job. I don't see that it will help her at all otherwise, and I don't want things getting any worse."

Emilio was quiet for a moment. He didn't want Sophia to feel like this kind of behaviour was acceptable, but equally, Sophia was an incredible chef, bringing in loads of business, and he didn't want to abandon her in the state she was in. It was a tough call. That was for sure.

Chapter 28

Sébastien Paris Pâtisserie, Val D'Isera Ski Resort, Austria: 4th December 2018

Audrey was feeling a lot calmer after her walk, but she was still frustrated with Violetta's attitude. If she'd had her way, Violetta would have got the sack long ago, but for some crazy reason, Stefan seemed attached to the girl and wouldn't let her go. When it came to choosing sides, he would always put Violetta's feelings above Audrey's, even though Audrey was his fiancée. Stefan said that it was simply a business decision and nothing personal. Besides, it wasn't like there was anyone else around to take on the job on such short notice and for as little as Stefan got away with paying Violetta.

Audrey threw her restaurant keys on the desk of the little office by the kitchen and spotted a printed greeting card with a picture of a teddy holding a heart and the words 'I'm So Sorry' on the front. It was the worst card Audrey had ever seen, cheap and tacky. She hated teddy bears. At least Stefan had tried to make up for taking Violetta's side in their argument earlier. She couldn't fault him for trying to put things right. What's more, he'd bought her a bunch of flowers and a bag of doughnuts.

Audrey was famished. She'd not eaten breakfast this morning, and then in all the commotion over the pineapple with Violetta storming out of the kitchen, Audrey had gone off for a long walk and spent most of the day crying her eyes out, trying to work out what to do to fix things. Now, as she got a wiff of the doughnuts, she realised how hungry she was. She pulled a doughnut from its bag and gobbled it down quickly. It tasted good, so she had a second, and then a third. She was about to pop the fourth one in her mouth, but she heard a noise in the seating area of the restaurant and went out to investigate.

It was Stefan, returned from his meeting, and he looked worn out as he loosened his tie and undid the top button on his shirt. "Oh, hey, babe," he called, smiling at her from across the room.

Audrey walked over to him and hugged him tightly. He smelt like old coffee and was hot and sweaty and unusually sticky.

"How did it go?" Audrey asked as she kissed him.

Stefan wasn't his usual affectionate self, and he was tired and irritable. It had been a rubbish day, and he didn't want the dramas or games or getting caught in the middle of Audrey's fights with other people. "Yeah, I think it went OK. How about you? Did you manage to get some fresh air and clear your head a bit?"

Audrey looked a bit miffed at his lack of interest in her. She had assumed from the flowers and doughnuts that he was apologising, but now she wasn't sure what was going on; he was giving her mixed signals. "Thanks for the card and flowers, Stefan. They're lovely, and the doughnuts are yummy too. I'm afraid I've almost eaten the whole bag of them already."

Stefan looked at her blankly, wondering if this was another of her games or her trying to catch him out. "Flowers? Card? I'm afraid they're nothing to do with me. I've been out all day." He wondered if he had walked right into a trap and perhaps should have bought her flowers and was now in for an ear-bashing. But he hadn't considered that he needed to buy her anything.

He had nothing to apologise for, and there was no special occasion.

"The flowers in the office? Look, I'll show you. If they're not from you, then who else would they be from?" Audrey led Stefan into the office and handed him the card.

"Well, they're nothing to do with me. Perhaps they're from one of your other boyfriends?" Stefan's comment could have been taken as a joke, but Audrey took it as an accusation. Even her fiancee was against her, and she had no idea why.

Stefan turned the card over. There was no message, no writing on it at all. He doubted that Violetta would get them for Audrey, but Violetta *had* said that she would do anything for him and knew how much of a headache the conflict between her and Audrey was causing him.

Stefan lied. "Well, they must be from Violetta then. She did say she was sorry that you'd fallen out this morning." He knew full well that Violetta would never apologise to Audrey, and as far as he was concerned, it was Audrey who had been bullying Violetta.

Audrey suddenly felt bad for thinking ill of Violetta. It was certainly nice of her to apologise like that. It couldn't have been easy, probably why she didn't do it in person.

"What happened to you?" Audrey asked Stefan as he took off his jacket and threw it on the back of the office chair. The light was better in the office than in the restaurant, and she could now see the coffee stains on his crisp white shirt.

Stefan did not want Audrey to find out about what had happened. It would only cause more friction between her and Sophia, and that would be bad for business. "Oh, it's a long and very dull story, nothing to write home about. I just spilt coffee down myself. A complete accident."

Audrey sensed that there was more to this story than Stefan was letting on. He was lying to her, but she would leave it for now. Things were already feeling very fractious between them. Best not to push them further.

"Well, I'd better go and get scrubbed up and into my chef gear. We'll be open soon, and I want to get a grip on things before the customers arrive."

"OK, honey," Stefan said as he shuffled some papers on his desk.

There was a sound at the back door as Violetta arrived for the start of her shift, and she popped her head around the office door. "Evening, boss."

Stefan turned to see Violetta and burst into hysterics as he saw her in a false wig and sunglasses. She was doing her best to cheer him up and to begin the shift on a more positive note. "Haha! You should wear that when you're working. Suits you."

Violetta bowed her imaginary cap at him. "Certainly, boss." She was about to turn around and begin work in the kitchen, but Stefan called her back.

"Oh, I wanted to say thanks, Violetta."

Violetta looked at him blankly from beneath her wig and sunglasses. "What for?"

Stefan tipped his head to the side. "You know what for. The flowers and card. It cheered Audrey up. I don't think you'll be getting any grief from her tonight." Stefan pointed to the card and flowers on the table."

Violetta snorted. "That'll be a first. I'll believe it when I see it. A shift with no fallouts with Audrey. Is that even possible?" Violetta smiled and went off to do her prep work before the guests arrived. She had no idea who the flowers and card were from, but if Stefan and Audrey believed they were from her, it made no sense to deny it, especially if it made the shift a little friendlier. She'd take the credit. What harm could come of it?

Stefan tidied up his desk and went upstairs to the apartment to change. He bumped into Audrey in the bedroom as she put on her chef whites. "You look awfully pale, Audrey. Are you alright?"

"Yes, I'm fine." Audrey lied. She was suddenly feeling tired and off-colour, but she assumed it was because she had barely eaten all day and had been under a lot of stress recently.

"There's one doughnut left in the office if you fancy it. I'm sure it's got your name on. Sugar might do you good."

Stefan pushed past her and pulled out his uniform as Audrey headed back downstairs to the kitchen, stopping in at the office to devour the last of the tasty doughnuts. She probably should have saved it for Violetta, but it was a bit late now as she'd already gobbled it down.

Audrey switched on the gas rings in the kitchen as the first of the evening's customers began to arrive. It wasn't long before orders for dishes were flooding in. Violetta was remarkably cheery, and for once they seemed to be getting along. Maybe Audrey had been wrong about Violetta? Perhaps she just needed encouragement rather than tough love?

"Is it just me, or is it really hot in here tonight?" Audrey asked Violetta as she grabbed the front of her chef top and wafted the air around her. She really must remember to eat regular meals in future; not eating all day was doing nothing to help her and they were in for a long night on their feet.

Violetta gave Audrey a worried look. "Are you feeling OK, Audrey? You do look a bit peaky. I can take over for a bit if you want to go and grab some air or something to eat."

Audrey's stomach suddenly somersaulted. "Yeah, you know what, that would be great. I'll be back in a bit." Audrey ran as fast as she could to the bathroom, suddenly aware that she needed the toilet. She got there just in time, but there was someone already in the locked bathroom. "Oh, come on," Audrey muttered under her breath as she clenched her butt cheeks together.

Finally, Audrey heard the latch on the door move, and out came her stepmother Margot looking quite anxious as she spoke on her phone. Margot was surprised to see Audrey and didn't stick around. Audrey rushed into the toilet and bolted the door behind her, hurrying to sit on the toilet.

She had awful diarrhoea and crippling stomach pains. She'd never had anything like this after eating doughnuts, but then again, it was unlike her not to eat for a whole day either. She doubled over, suddenly feeling very nauseous. It must be food poisoning, she thought as she held her fingers to her neck to check her pulse. Or maybe she was just being a hysterical wreck.

Audrey could feel her heart beating against her chest, and it seemed to be slowing down. She felt oddly scared, but couldn't leave the toilet, or call anyone since her phone was in the office near the kitchen. She would just have to hope that one of the customers came to use the toilet soon so that she could call out to them to get their attention. She summoned all her strength and managed to unbolt the door, opening it before feeling as if she might just pass out. Her head was starting to throb. Something was very, very wrong indeed.

Part Seven

A Turn for the Worse

Chapter 29

Sébastien Paris Pâtisserie, Val D'Isera Ski Resort, Austria: 4th December 2018

Stefan changed as quickly as he could and arrived in the kitchen, impressed to see Violetta taking over much of the cooking responsibility. "Well, look at you being all helpful," he said, smiling at Violetta's efforts.

Violetta seemed to be cross. "Well, I thought I would do my best to be helpful, so I offered to mind the pots, but Audrey's disappeared just like she always does, leaving me to do everything on my own. She's been gone for ages."

Stefan looked perplexed. Sure, Audrey pushed Violetta to work hard, but no more than in any other kitchen of this ilk. Audrey took great pride in her cooking and demanded perfection, so if she was taking a break, he knew there would be a very good reason for it. "Well, how long has she been gone exactly? Did she say where she was going?"

Violetta shrugged. "I dunno. Twenty or thirty minutes, maybe. Said she was going for some fresh air."

"Well, that's weird." Stefan looked at the long line of white papers pinned to the shelf. This was a disaster. They were already behind on the orders, and the customers would not be happy at all. This was the last thing he needed.

There was a knock on the kitchen door, and Margot appeared with a bunch of papers in her hand, closely followed by Rose. They both looked very determined.

"Where's Audrey?" Margot demanded as she glanced around the kitchen. I simply can't wait; she must sign these papers immediately. No more avoiding me.

"No, she does not have to sign them," added Rose. "Stefan, you must get Audrey to make a decision once and for all."

Stefan lost his cool with the two ladies. "Well, if I could flippin' find Audrey, then I'd tell her, but right now she's gone AWOL."

"What do you mean, 'gone AWOL?'" Rose asked, "I saw her about half an hour ago going towards the toilet, just as Margot was coming out."

"Is that true? Did you see her in the toilet?" Stefan asked Margot.

"No, it's not true at all. Someone was waiting to go in after I came out, but they were in a hurry, and I was distracted, so I didn't pay any attention. I suppose it *could* have been Audrey, now that you mention it."

Rose waved her finger at Margot, suddenly cross. "If you've done anything to harm Audrey, you'll be ever so sorry," Rose threatened.

Margot looked horrified. "Done anything? Done anything? What do you think I am? Some kind of serial killer? My own step-daughter?"

Stefan was suddenly unsure about Margot. "Well, it's no secret that the two of you have been arguing a lot recently, is it? You don't exactly seem maternal towards her."

IT HADN'T TAKEN Camilla and Emilio long to figure out that they quite liked each other, and they soon started to spend time together, much to

Francesca's disgust. Emilio had invited them both to join him at the restaurant for dinner, a kind of date—with the daughter in tow—but also a way to show Stefan that he was sorry about what had happened in the coffee shop and that he wanted his business to thrive. If people saw Emilio dining at the restaurant, they would be less likely to think that the two business owners had fallen out, which would result in better outcomes for both men.

Emilio poured them a glass of wine and finished off his course. They were already feeling quite full. Camilla was keen for Francesca to get to know Emilio, so she made the excuse of going to powder her nose, giving her daughter and new boyfriend a moment to get to know each other without her being around to make either of them feel awkward.

It didn't take Camilla long to realise that all was not well as she pushed open the toilet door and saw Audrey's lifeless body lying on the floor. She let out a scream, suddenly feeling overcome and rather faint, just as Stefan, Violetta, Rose, and Margot raced along the corridor and saw the body for themselves.

Rose escorted Camilla back to her table with Francesca and Emilio and poured her a large glass of whisky, giving her orders to stay put.

Emilio was shocked at the news, but not

surprised when he heard rumours from the other guests that Audrey had been murdered. He was only glad that he had sent Sophia home early from work, so at least she wouldn't get accused of harming Audrey. She was sure to be the number one suspect after her little outburst in his coffee shop today.

"Emilio, Stefan's asked if you can give Dr Sim a call; do you have his number?" Rose asked, clearly running on adrenaline. She was certain that if it was murder, Margot was behind it, and she didn't want to leave Margot anywhere near the body for fear that Margot might destroy the evidence and get away with it.

Emilio pulled out his phone. He had stored the doctor's number in case it was ever needed for one of his customers after a slip or fall on ice in the street, or a sprained ankle on a skier. Little did he imagine he'd be calling the resort's main medic to the scene of a suspected murder. Sim was a regular customer at the coffee shop, liked to order the iced drinks, no matter what the weather. Nice guy. Irish and a bit of a scruff, spoke a million miles an hour. Emilio tapped in the number and let it ring.

"Hullo, Dr Sim MacDiar speaking. Is that you, Emilio? Saw your name pop up on the screen there. What can I do you for?"

"Hey, Sim. Not sure how to tell you this, but we need you to come to Stefan's restaurant as soon as you can. Audrey's been found dead in the toilet. There's talk of murder, but I've not seen the body myself."

"Are you sure she's dead and not just passed out?" Sim enquired.

Emilio had no reason to doubt the witnesses when they said that Audrey was dead, but he didn't want to look like an idiot either. "As I say, I've not seen the body myself, but the witnesses are in agreement about her being dead, so chances are she probably is."

"No bother. I'll be there in two ticks, alright?" Sim hung up the phone, leaving Stefan's mind racing and trying to piece events together.

"Doesn't it seem a bit odd that everyone says it's a murder?" Francesca asked to no one in particular. "I mean, surely the most likely thing would be that she died of natural causes, I don't know, like a heart attack or a subarachnoid haemorrhage? How does everyone know that it was murder and not natural causes that killed her?"

"You know what, that's a very good point that you make there, Francesca," Emilio agreed.

It wasn't long until Bastian Rainer, the local police officer, arrived at the restaurant and was busy with his two junior officers making notes and looking around the scene of the crime. He interviewed all the guests, took down their details, and allowed them to leave, focusing on only the main suspects, of which there seemed to be many. It was going to be a very long night.

Chapter 30

Sébastien Paris Pâtisserie, Val D'Isera Ski Resort, Austria: 4th December 2018

"And you are … ?" Bastian asked his first suspect, taking out a small notebook and pencil, and scribbling details as he went about his informal questioning.

"Violetta. I'm the kitchen porter here."

"And how was your relationship with the deceased?" Bastian glanced over the top of his bifocal glasses, trying to determine whether Violetta was indeed his killer, as Stefan had hinted at.

Violetta knew she was in a great deal of trouble, even though she had done nothing wrong. She just hoped that if she told the officer the truth, everything would get sorted out sooner or later.

"We had a bit of a love-hate relationship, I suppose. We had a falling out this morning, but then we made up this evening and were getting along better than we've ever done before."

"Would you say that's correct?" Bastian asked Stefan as they all stood in the kitchen.

"Yes, I'd say that was a pretty accurate summary. They did fall out this morning, but then they made up as far as I'm aware. Violetta left a card, flowers, and some doughnuts for Audrey by way of an apology, and Audrey was chuffed to bits with them."

Bastian scribbled some more. "And what exactly did you fall out about?"

Violetta sighed. "To be honest, it all feels a bit silly now, but we were both angry at the time. We fell out because I cut up the pineapple wrongly, and Audrey threw it in the bin. It was petty, I know."

Stefan felt he needed to justify Violetta's actions. "I'd say it was fairly usual for staff to fall out over such seemingly trivial things when working in top-rated restaurants. Especially with chefs being perfectionists. Though I was surprised that Violetta sent gifts as an apology."

Violetta's heart suddenly felt heavy, like it

might just stop completely. It had seemed like a good idea to take credit for sending those flowers and card, but her lies could now get her in a lot of serious trouble. She tried hard to avert her gaze from the police officer's eyes, suddenly feeling like a criminal. "You see the thing is, well, OK, I lied about sending the flowers and card, and I didn't know anything about there being doughnuts. I just saw how happy the idea of me sending them to Audrey made you, Stefan, so I went along with it. It was a stupid white lie, but I truly didn't realise I'd be getting in this much trouble because of it. I ... I ... I just wanted to make you happy."

"Well, it certainly wasn't me who sent them, so one of us must be lying," Stefan pointed out to the police officer.

Chapter 31

Disco Diva Bar and Club, Val D'Isera Ski
Resort, Austria: 4th December 2018

"This is great!" Eloise shouted at me across
the dance floor of the resort's nightclub
and bar.

We were both hot from dancing, and I was
quite looking forward to a rest after my early start
of baking at the coffee shop. Eloise, on the other
hand, was full of energy and very hyperactive. I
leant towards her, shouting so she could hear me
above the music. "I need a break! I'm going to sit
down for a bit."

"OK." Eloise followed me as I walked towards
the bar where Nicklas sat sulking. It was a shame

Violetta was never able to join him at the club. As always, she was working at the restaurant, and it would be several hours before she got to go home. It was rare that she and Nicklas found time to spend together, especially since Nicklas was up early preparing for his day on the slopes. It must have been hard for them both.

Karl would usually have been able to cheer Nicklas up, but tonight he was rushed off his feet, serving the latest trend in ski bar cocktails. He heated a large saucepan of liquid and poured the boiling liquor into several small, ceramic cups on the bar as a group of Italians watched expectantly. He was quite the showman, and he worked quickly. Karl pulled out a box of matches and struck one on the side as it caught alight. Karl wafted the flame above the cups and they quickly sprang to life, burning brightly with their blue flames. The Italian ski party cheered and reached in for a cup each as Karl tidied up the mess.

"Wow, what's that?" I asked him.

Karl ran the back of his hand across his brow to mop up some of the sweat. "Parampampoli. It's all the rage at the moment. Loads of people have been asking for it, and once you make one, suddenly everyone else wants one. Going to be a busy night at this rate. I've already lost count of how many I've made."

"What's in it? I asked; I was always on the lookout for new flavours for my coffee shop bakes.

"It's pretty simple, really," Karl replied. "Just espresso, red wine, grappa, brandy, honey. Oh, and some sugar."

I'd never tried grappa before, and I decided to ask Karl later whether he could tell me a bit more about it and maybe spare some for me to experiment in the coffee shop. We set fire to our Christmas puddings with our Christmas dinner each holiday at home in England, and having seen how impressed the crowd was with the flames, I wondered if I might begin a range of flaming bakes.

"I'm sure I can hear a phone ringing." Eloise looked around her and stuck a finger in her ear, wondering if it might be just her ear buzzing from the loud music on the dance floor.

"It's not me. I forgot my phone completely," I said, looking around. I thought I could hear a phone ringing too.

"Don't look at me." Karl threw up his hands to declare his innocence. "I'd get fired on the spot if the boss caught me with my phone on a shift. Mine's switched off in the drawer down there."

Nicklas almost fell off his stool as he pulled out his phone from his back pocket. "I think it's mine, but no one ever calls me, and Violetta's at work so it can't be her." It was a withheld number. Nicklas looked mystified; the only people who ever called him were Karl and Violetta, and it wouldn't be either of them since both were currently on shifts with bosses who banned their employees from using phones at work.

It was a bad line, and it took Nicklas a while to recognise the voice on the other end of the phone. "Hello? Hello? Who is this? Who's calling? I'm afraid I can't hear you very well; the line's awful." He pulled the phone from his ear and fumbled for the volume button on the side. "Hello? That's a bit better; I can hear you a little more clearly. Violetta? Is that you? Wait, I thought you were at work?"

I could see from Nicklas's face that he was distressed. I didn't need to be in the clear light of day to recognise that his face had become pale suddenly, even with us being in a dark club.

He steadied himself with a hand on the edge of the bar. "It's Violetta," he whispered to us as we waited for further information. He spoke again to Violetta. "Shit. I can't believe it. Are you for real? Why would they think that? Violetta? Violetta? Wait, give me your number; I think my battery is about to die. Of course, I'll come and get you."

Karl passed him a scrap of paper and a pencil

as Nicklas frantically wrote down a phone number. "Got it. I'll call you back in two secs. Don't go anywhere."

Nicklas shoved his dead phone in his back pocket and looked desperately at his brother. "Karl, I need to use your phone to call Violetta. It's an emergency."

Eloise and I looked at each other for a moment. Whatever was going on, it sounded very serious.

"Come on, mate. I'm dying of thirst over here!" a drunk man called over to Karl, who was so caught up in the moment that he had neglected his bar customers.

"In the drawer, bro; help yourself. You know my phone lock code, right?" Karl walked along the bar and took the drunk man's drink order, leaving Nicklas to rummage around the drawer. But he couldn't see Karl's phone anywhere.

"Oh, come on. Seriously!" Nicklas muttered as he rifled through the drawer. He was shaking with the fear of what he had just heard from Violetta and couldn't make head nor tail of things as he desperately tried to find Karl's phone.

Seeing he was distressed, I offered to help him and moved him to one side as I crept behind the bar and looked in the drawer myself.

"There it is!" I exclaimed, passing the phone

to Nicklas. It was right on top. But my eye was distracted by something else in the drawer, something very sparkly, that was covered in diamonds. I grabbed hold of the object, not quite believing my eyes. I held it up to inspect it more closely.

"Wait! Isn't that Audrey's watch?" Eloise observed.

I thought Nicklas might faint at any moment, and he lost all power of his muscles, dropping Karl's phone on the floor. "It can't be!"

I quickly closed the drawer and rushed to Nicklas's side as Eloise and I tried hard to steady him. "What is it, Nicklas? What's going on?" I asked, not especially wanting to hear whatever it was that had got Nicklas so full of fear.

Nicklas reached his hand to his jaw in an attempt to make his lower jaw reconnect with the rest of his face. "Audrey's dead."

I shoved the watch in my pocket, thinking I had misheard. "Dead?" I mouthed.

Nicklas was struggling to speak and seemed to be only capable of single words right now. "Murdered."

"Wait. What?" I spluttered.

If Audrey had been murdered, then there were two obvious suspects in my mind right now. One of them was Karl because the dead girl's watch had turned up in his drawer at his workplace, and Violetta who, as Nicklas's girlfriend also had access and knowledge of the drawer behind the bar, and had turned up unexpectedly at the glacier the day that someone tried to kill Audrey and when the watch had gone missing.

Nicklas fumbled and picked up the dropped phone, and grabbed at the scrap of paper with the number for Violetta on it. She had been very distressed on the phone and he had, after all, promised to call her right back. "Violetta," he said in haste.

Eloise misunderstood Nicklas's meaning. "Do you really think Violetta did it? But she's your girlfriend. Surely?"

Nicklas looked annoyed. "Of course, Violetta wouldn't do it. That's not what I meant. But I must phone her back. She's been arrested, but she says she is innocent. They're accusing her of giving Audrey the doughnuts that killed her."

"Oh, my God!" I cried, suddenly realising that I too might be a suspect in the case. I was after all the main person at the resort baking doughnuts. What if Audrey had been killed by a doughnut; what if it had come from Emilio's coffee shop, baked by *me*?

Eloise grabbed my arm. "What is it, Maddy?

What's wrong?" I didn't want to share my concerns in front of Nicklas right now and make things worse. "Nothing. I'll tell you later, OK. But we need to get to the station, see if we can help solve the case and clear Violetta's name."

Chapter 32

Interview Room, Val D'Isera Police Station,
Austria: 4th December 2018

Violetta sat very still and quiet at the
interrogation desk in the small, confined
room. She wasn't sure what the room
was called, but it sure felt like an interrogation.

The police officer switched on the recorder.
"This is Bastian Rainer of the Val D'Isera Police
Department interviewing suspect Violetta Gruca
at 11 pm on the 4th December 2018. For the
purposes of the recording, can you please confirm
your name."

"Violetta Gruca," whispered Violetta, her
mouth suddenly dry.

Bastian asked Violetta question after question

about the events of the day, leaving out no detail at all. "Are you in the habit of lying, Miss Gruca? Would you say that's a fair statement?"

"What? No, of course not. I'm not a liar."

Bastian continued his probing. "Let me get this straight. You say that you are not a liar, and yet not sixty minutes ago, you confessed to me at the restaurant that you had lied about giving the card, flowers, and doughnuts to Audrey by way of an apology. So, which is it to be? Are you a liar, or aren't you? It's a very simple question."

Violetta was agitated. It didn't matter what she said; this Bastian would only twist her words to mean something else. "Look. I'm not a liar. But I did tell a small white lie today. But it was only because I wanted to make someone else happy, to stop them from suffering."

"So, did you or did you not give the card, flowers, and doughnuts to Audrey?" Bastian repeated.

"I did *not* give them to Audrey, nor did I leave them on the desk for her to find. I simply did not correct Stefan when he suggested that I had left them there as a peace offering for Audrey."

There was a knock at the door, and a second police officer popped his head into the room. "A word please, sir."

Bastian cleared his throat. "For the tape,

Officer Bianco has asked me to step out of the interview room for a moment."

IT DIDN'T TAKE us long to get to the police station, and we were quick to give our names and involvement in the case to the police officer at the desk. He eyed us rather suspiciously and called one of the officers.

"Take a seat, please. Officer Bianco will be with you shortly." The officer at the desk pointed Nicklas, Eloise, and I to a row of plastic seats in the waiting area, and the three of us sat in silence, processing the events of the day.

"Where's Violetta? Is she OK? Can I see her?" Nicklas babbled as the desk officer approached us. "Not just yet, I'm afraid. We need to interview you separately first, to see if we can shed more light on events."

Officer Bianco interviewed Eloise and Nicklas first, and I began to grow very anxious as I waited for my turn. It felt like hours had passed by the time I was finally called in for my interview.

I found myself fidgeting with my fingers as Officer Bianco sat and stared at me in silence. I was sure he was trying to psyche me out. The officer pulled out a photo. "Do you know what these are?"

Of course, I did, I had slaved over them for hours this morning. I looked at him in earnest.

"Yes, sir. Those are doughnuts, more specifically, they are the red velvet doughnuts that I baked myself this morning at the coffee shop, I'd recognise them anywhere."

The officer seemed surprised that I had admitted it so easily. He'd expected at least a bit of resistance before I made my confession.

BASTIAN RETURNED to the interview room and re-started the recording. "For the purposes of the tape, I'm showing Miss Gruca Exhibit A." Bastian placed the photo of the doughnuts in front of Violetta. "Do you know what these are?"

It seemed like a trick question. Anyone could see that they were doughnuts. Violetta shrugged her shoulders. "Doughnuts?"

"Don't try and be funny with me, miss," Bastian complained, feeling as if Violetta was trying to play dumb but was, in fact, Audrey's cold and calculating murderer. "Where did you get them from?

Violetta blinked. "I didn't get them from anywhere. I've never seen them before in my life."

"Don't try and pull the wool over my eyes, missy. You know exactly where they came from, don't you?" Bastian was growing tired of Violetta's avoidance of admitting that she killed Audrey.

"Look." Violetta gave a huge sigh of frustration. "I'm telling you. I've NEVER seen these before. All I can tell you is that yes, they do look like doughnuts, but beyond that, I have nothing to add. If you need a doughnut expert, then I suggest you speak to Madeleine Cooke."

Finally, Bastian felt like he might be getting somewhere. "Madeleine Cooke? Why do you say that?"

Violetta shook her head in sheer amazement. This Bastian couldn't have been a very good policeman if he didn't know who to speak to about doughnuts in the small ski resort. "Are you for real? Everyone knows that if you want a doughnut expert, you go to see Madeleine. Surely you've seen the queues outside the coffee shop when people know she's baking."

Bastian had often wondered why there was always a crowd outside the coffee shop first thing in the morning. It had never occurred to him that it might be people waiting to get their doughnuts.

Personally, he didn't care for cakes and pastries very much, and he saw people who ate them or who drank coffee as being weak-willed. He was more of a carrot stick and hummus man himself. Far better for you, and without the calories. He liked to treat his body as a temple.

I WAITED for Officer Bianco to ask me another question, but he seemed to look a bit scared by me.

"Just a moment," he said. "I'll be back shortly."

Officer Bianco kept looking at me sideways as he left the interview room. It seemed as if he was nervous that I might suddenly do him in. He was still looking right at me as he blindly fumbled for the handle on the door and reversed out of it, not wanting to have his back to me. He was a very nervous and strange chap.

I sat in silence, staring at the blank walls and ceiling of the poky room. It could certainly do with a fresh lick of paint and a few pictures to brighten the place up. Officer Bianco returned with another officer, and the two of them slumped into seats on the opposite side of the little table facing me, both with arms folded.

I waited and watched them, expecting them to say something, but they seemed to be a bit lost for words. I wanted to say something to break the ice, but I couldn't think of anything appropriate right now, so I tried to keep my expression as straight and neutral as I could, for fear that I might burst out laughing as I watched the eyebrows on the new officer dance about on his face as he thought whatever it was he was thinking.

After some time, he finally spoke. "Right then, missy, let's be having you. What are these? And don't be telling me doughnuts. I know they are doughnuts." The officer, Bastian, as I later learnt he was called, handed me the same photo that Officer Bianco had shown me. It was hard to think of what to say, because he had asked me what they were, and I had wanted to say they were doughnuts because that's what they were. If I said anything else, I'd have been lying.

"Well?" I answered. "These are red velvet doughnuts, and I cooked up a huge batch of them this morning right before the coffee shop opened."

"Did you now?" Bastian commented.

I pulled a funny face without meaning to. "That's what I just said. I'm not denying that I baked these doughnuts this morning. I can tell they are mine because they have my signature letter 'm' right there in icing. It's my little trademark." I pointed to the tiny letter on the side of the doughnut.

"And did you at any point give these doughnuts to Audrey?" Bastian asked.

I thought about it for a moment, realising that I needn't have been worried at all. I hadn't even seen Audrey, let alone given her one of my doughnuts, and I certainly hadn't poisoned them. "I've not seen Audrey at all today, but her fiancé Stefan did come into the coffee shop, which he very rarely does, and he was dressed in a fancy business suit and got into a nasty argument with our pot washer Sophia. She's the one who taught me this recipe. She's a pastry chef really, but Audrey stole her job from her at Sebastian's restaurant." I feared that I might have said too much, and I didn't want to get anyone else in trouble. But it was too late.

Officer Bianco was frantically scribbling down notes, trying to keep up with me as I spilt all my knowledge to him and tried to piece the events of the day together.

"And how did Stefan seem to you? Was he angry with Sophia?" Bastian asked.

It was an odd thing to ask, and it now seemed strange to me that Stefan had not been angry at all, given the circumstances. "Actually, he was quite alright with things. Didn't seem to be much

236

bothered. He even asked Emilio, my boss, not to give Sophia a hard time or to fire her for throwing the coffee over him. He was so nice about things that Emilio decided to give him a bag of my doughnuts to take with him to enjoy with Audrey. You can ask Emilio yourself if you need proof."

Officer Bianco looked up from his notes for a moment, before scribbling down some more. He wrote the name Emilio in capital letters and drew several lines underneath the name to highlight it as if it were somehow significant. It didn't occur to me at the time that in explaining what had happened, I had somehow incriminated Emilio in the process.

It took a long time to recollect all the events of the day, and when I got to the part about sitting in the nightclub and finding Audrey's watch, I wondered whether I should say anything at all because I doubted very much that Karl might be the murderer. But I felt it was my duty as a future detective to tell them everything I knew.

Part Eight

The Detectives are on the Case

Chapter 33

Snow Mountain Coffee Shop, Val D'Isera Ski Resort, Austria: 5th December 2018

With news of Audrey's murder and Madeleine and Eloise being held at the police station overnight for questioning, there were very few customers at the coffee shop that morning. But plenty of people were peering through the coffee shop window or hanging around outside on the pavement, hoping to catch sight of some arrests. Emilio looked glum. It was hard to know who to trust these days.

"I'm sure it'll all be fine," Théo said to console Emilio. "And for what it's worth, I don't think for a moment that Maddy or Eloise is guilty. Chances are the police will figure that out too very soon."

Théo called Sophia over to help provide some reassurance to Emilio. "Wouldn't you agree, Sophia? There's no way that Madeleine or Eloise would harm anyone."

Sophia said nothing.

Emilio threw his head into his hands. "Oh God. Don't tell me you think the girls are guilty too?"

Sophia made as if she were reluctantly offering her opinion on the matter. "I'm afraid that the evidence does rather overwhelming point to Madeleine committing the murder." She said. "You can't avoid the facts, can you?"

Théo was curious to hear Sophia's take on the subject. "In what way, Sophia?"

Sophia piped up again, a little too keenly for Théo's liking. "Well, it's obvious, isn't it? The girls are desperate to set up their detective agency and they needed to have some murders to work on to help them build their reputation. You only have to look at that stash of detective and forensics books in their room at the chalet. I've never seen so many books about poisoning and how to catch a killer. That's not normal behaviour, is it?"

Théo laughed. "You can hardly use the possession of textbooks as evidence for a murder, Sophia. The girls are off to university to study forensics and criminology next year. I expect they just want to read all the course textbooks before they arrive. Nothing wrong with that, is there?"

"Hey, you asked my opinion and I gave it. I just think it's odd that Audrey died after eating doughnuts that we all know Madeleine baked. She is the queen of the doughnuts, after all. Everyone says it."

Chapter 34

Interview Room, Val D'Isera Police Station, Austria: 5th December 2018

"How much longer are you going to keep me here?" Violetta asked the police officer.

Bastian pushed his slipping glasses back to where they belonged. "I'm going to release you, but don't think that means you got away with it. It just means that we haven't found enough evidence against you *yet*. But I'm working on it, so don't go leaving town anytime soon."

Violetta wanted to cry, partly from anger and partly from relief. "Well, good luck with that. I'm innocent, so I doubt that you'll find anything incriminating against me."

Bastian opened the door to the interview room and pointed Violetta towards the exit. Violetta turned to him, not quite sure what to do now she had been set free. "How am I supposed to get home? You wouldn't let me pick up my things when you brought me in from the restaurant. I've not got my wallet, phone or anything with me. I'm not even wearing my proper clothes. Do you expect me to freeze to death in the snow?"

Violetta looked down at her kitchen overalls. She felt quite horrid in them after a full day of prepping in the kitchen, followed by a shift washing pots and portering, and more recently a night in the cells and interrogation room.

The police officer wasn't sympathetic to her plight. "Not my problem. Can't you call someone to pick you up?"

"I would, but you brought them in for questioning, remember?" Violetta shook her head in disbelief.

Violetta wasn't even sure who she could call to come and get her. Audrey was dead, Stefan would be grieving, Eloise, Nicklas, and Maddy were still being detained at the station, and besides, she didn't have a phone on her. The only person she could call was Karl, but he didn't have transport, and he'd probably be sleeping after his shift. She'd simply have to wait in the reception area until the others were released. She curled up on the reception room chairs and quickly fell asleep.

BASTIAN CALLED Eloise and I from our cramped police cell and brought us into the interview room, this time together, which was a lot less daunting than being interviewed on our own.

"Right, then. I've had a very interesting anonymous call about you being the most likely suspect for this murder. It isn't looking good for you; I'll be honest." Bastian smirked, pleased with himself for being close to solving his first murder case. He didn't know what the fuss was about. Crime-solving was hardly difficult. "Now, tell me about these books of yours."

I was confused for a moment, and from Eloise's face, she seemed as stumped as me. "Books?" I enquired.

"Yes, books. The ones in your bedroom at the chalet, all about poisons and forensic psychology and criminology. Don't go denying it. I've got proof." Bastian held up a book in a sealed plastic bag. I recognised it immediately. It was the one that my parents had got me for my birthday and was entitled *Forensic Psychology for Beginners*. I couldn't help but stifle a laugh as I recalled the words that my parents had written inside:

To our darling daughter, we saw this book and thought of you. Hope it helps you with your criminal masterminding. Lots of love, Mum and Dad xxx

I knew at once who the anonymous tip-off was from. It was from Sophia. She was the only one in the chalet with access to our girls' quarters, and I'd found one of my poisons books hidden amongst a pile of her laundry. I wouldn't have known about it if it weren't for me being clumsy and knocking over her chair as I tried to pull on my salopettes in the dark for an early morning ski.

Bastian looked at us with beady eyes. "So, what did you poison her with then? Come on, spill."

We were both quiet, not quite knowing what to say. Bastian continued his line of enquiry.

"What was it then? Arsenic? Rat poison? Snake venom?"

It was Eloise's turn to snigger a little, and I was having trouble controlling my twisted sense of humour too. "Poppycock," Eloise spluttered, unable to control herself.

The police officer was understandably growing tired of us, but it was difficult to be serious around a man who had watched too many murder mysteries on the telly. We were both innocent. But Bastian had already made up his mind. *We* had killed Audrey.

Eloise pulled herself together as best as she could. "If we were going to kill anyone, then I doubt very much that we would poison them, and if we were to poison them, then we would certainly not do it using arsenic or rat poison or anything like that."

Bastian felt like he was making headway at last, and he rubbed his hands together with glee. "Go on."

I tried as best I could to keep things simple for him. "You see, the thing is, there are very few poisons that leave no trace in the system, so most poisons would be picked up on an autopsy. Poison would be a sure way to leave traces and get yourself caught for it."

Eloise continued my line of thought. "And it's a common myth that poisons kill quickly and are undetectable, so poison really wouldn't be the way to go if we wanted to murder someone and get away with it."

"Are you admitting that you murdered someone then?" Bastian asked, suddenly excited. "So, you're saying that you *wanted* to get caught, that's why you used poison?"

I rolled my eyes. "You're not listening to me. Audrey died within a few hours of eating the doughnuts, right?"

Bastian nodded.

"Well then, if we were to use arsenic, we would need to be giving it to her over several weeks for it to kill her, and she would be unwell for weeks before she died. But we've only been here for just over a week, so we couldn't have killed her with arsenic." I was about to mention that we had met her once in the summer at our party, but that would just make things worse right now. Overcomplicate things.

Bastian interjected before I had time to mention the summer party anyway, "But what about rat poison?"

Eloise leant forward. "If we had killed her with rat poison, she would have died a quick and messy death with very different symptoms, apart from which it would have been very difficult to administer to her without her noticing. She would have tasted it immediately, and we didn't even see her all day."

There was a sudden knock on the door that made Eloise and I jump as we remembered that we were being accused of murdering Audrey. I rather hoped that the officer who entered the room might have come to tell us that it had all been a big misunderstanding, but it was not to be.

"I need a quick word with you, sir, if you don't mind. I've got the initial toxicology report back."

Bastian looked triumphant. "Ha! Now we'll find out what you used to poison her with."

The officer who had knocked on the door left as quickly as he had arrived, followed by Bastian.

"Do you have any idea who murdered Audrey?" I asked Eloise now that we were alone again.

"I've got my suspicions, but I just don't know how we can prove it yet," Eloise replied.

Bastian came back into the room and sat down at the interview table, switching the recorder back on. "It seems I quite underestimated you both. You're much cleverer than I first anticipated." Bastian looked down at a piece of paper he was holding. "To be honest, you might have got away with this, but nothing gets past the Val D'Isera police department."

Eloise and I looked at each other, none the wiser.

"Very clever indeed. Cerbera odollam. Better known as the Suicide Tree. The perfect murder weapon. I bet you never thought we would run a toxicology report on that, did you?"

"I've never heard of it, have you?" I asked Eloise.

"It doesn't sound familiar," Eloise replied.

Bastian did look pleased with himself. Not only did he believe he had solved the murder, but he had discovered that the murder weapon was very rare and especially difficult to trace. He was sure to get an award and a nice big pay rise for his sleuthing abilities from the police commissioner.

"Hats off to you both. Really, I mean it. I'm impressed. According to my man in the toxicology department, you can eat the fruit, but the seed itself is deadly. He reckons that you grated the nut finely and added it to the doughnuts. You'll be going down a long time for this."

Eloise suddenly had a flash of inspiration as she remembered something that Emilio had said on our first day at the coffee shop, but she couldn't believe for a minute that Emilio was the murderer, and she didn't want him to get in trouble either. But she had no choice. "Maddy, I've thought of something."

"What is it?" I asked.

Eloise hesitated. "You remember our very first day in the coffee shop when Emilio showed us his secret stash of beans? Well, there was something in one of the jars that he said was poisonous as a nut, but that the fruit itself was perfectly safe and tasty to eat."

I remembered. "Oh, yeah. The beans he got on his trip to India in the summer."

"Yes, that's the one." Eloise nodded.

We looked at Bastian, who suddenly seemed deflated, at least until the part where we mentioned Emilio having a secret stash of beans. That seemed to appeal to Bastian's sense of importance, and he quickly changed his tune.

Bastian thought hard. If he could catch this Emilio, then not only would the murderer have been caught, but he could reduce the risks of heart disease and diabetes amongst the resort visitors too. The coffee shop would have to close, and no one would be able to indulge in cakes, pastries, and coffee anymore. There would be less rubbish on the streets without people dumping coffee cups and paper bags everywhere.

"Emilio, you say? And where exactly is this secret stash of beans?" Bastian asked.

I felt the need to try and put things into context a bit before Bastian got ahead of himself again. "Well, he calls them his secret stash of beans, but that's more for fun. They're not really secret."

"And who has access to these beans?" Bastian enquired.

I looked at Eloise as I tried to recall and not forget anyone. "Well, that would be Emilio, me, Eloise, and Sophia. No one else."

"Very well," Bastian said as he escorted Eloise and I back to our holding cell and locked the door.

ELOISE LEANT AGAINST THE WALL, and I rested my head on her knees. "Let's look at this from a new angle, just for the sake of argument, make sure we aren't missing any obvious clues here," Eloise suggested. "What motive does Emilio have for murdering Audrey?"

I racked my brains, struggling to find a reason. "Well, I suppose the restaurant is the only competition for the coffee shop."

Eloise frowned. "But that makes no sense at all. The coffee shop has been doing brilliantly since we arrived, and Sophia's and your baking has brought in a lot of extra revenue. If anything, the coffee shop is taking business away from the restaurant, not the other way around, but I don't even think that is the case."

I listened carefully, processing my thoughts and Eloise's ideas. "If that was the situation, then the most likely outcome would be Stefan murdering Sophia or trying to frame Emilio for the murder to get rid of the competition. Why would Stefan kill his award-winning pastry chef?"

Eloise stretched out her arms against the cold, hard walls of the cell. "Unless Emilio was having a secret affair with Violetta and he wanted revenge for the way that Audrey treated Violetta in the workplace."

I wondered that too, but it just seemed ridiculous. "Beats me. I don't see any reason at all why Emilio might murder Audrey. Unless it has something to do with Théo, but I've got no means or motive there either."

Chapter 35

Snow Mountain Café, Val D'Isera Ski Resort,
Austria: 5th December 2018

Bastian entered the coffee shop with an over-inflated sense of self-worth. He had expected there to be at least a few people present to witness his great detecting skills. Rumour had led him to believe that the coffee shop was popular, and he had himself seen the long queues outside when passing in his police car. But alas, there was no one here today, just a solitary customer, who had his head buried in the crossword of the local newspaper, and a man standing behind the coffee counter.

He strutted over to the till eager to see what this Emilio character was like.

"Can I help you?" Emilio enquired.

Bastian puffed out his chest and dusted off his epaulettes. "I'm looking for a man by the name of Emilio Silvestre. He's a suspect in our murder enquiry. Have you seen him?"

Emilio thought the strange police officer might be joking for a second. "Um, sure. Yes, that's me. I'm Emilio Silvestre. But I didn't know I was a suspect. That's the first I've heard of it."

Sophia appeared from the kitchen behind the counter, along with Théo, who had dropped his crossword, eager to hear more about Emilio's suspected criminal activities.

"I've cause to believe that you have a secret room filled with murderous poisons," Bastian announced as two police officers arrived in the coffee shop and stood next to him, shoulder to shoulder. "I'm here to search your premises."

Emilio looked at the three officers. There was no way that they were going to have access to his collection of beautiful beans, some of them from trees and plants that were now extinct. He didn't trust them to take care of the neatly arranged jars or to understand their worth, not just to him, but to the world. He knew he would get into trouble, but he couldn't put his collection in harm's way.

"Secret stash of poisons? No, sorry, I can't

258

help you there." It wasn't exactly a lie; he didn't have any secret stash of 'murderous poisons.'

"They're through here," Sophia told Bastian. "Follow me."

Théo looked horrified. "Sophia? What are you playing at?"

Bastian followed Sophia into the storeroom and watched her as she entered the code on the keypad. There was a click, and she opened the vault door fully. She was a pretty young lady, and he was most appreciative of her kindness and good nature. He mentally ruled her out as a suspect in his enquiries. A girl like that could never hurt a fly.

"Thank you for your help and cooperation, Miss — "

Sophia held out her hand to him, and Bastian kissed it. What a charming lady indeed. "Sophia Saner. Pleased to meet you, sir."

Bastian was quite taken with the girl's perfume and her accent. "French?" he asked, entranced.

Sophia smiled sweetly. "Yes, Paris."

"Very good," said Bastian.

Sophia pointed at the many shelves filled with jars. "Here, these are the beans. Are you looking for anything in particular?"

Bastian was by now confident that Sophia was not his killer. He had been eavesdropping on

Madeleine and Eloise in the police cell, and they had talked about how they thought Sophia was the most likely murderer, but Bastian couldn't see it himself. "Perhaps you can help me. I'm looking for Cerbera odollam."

Sophia smiled again, trying hard to look like she wasn't very bright. "Well, I know that Emilio likes to arrange the jars in alphabetical order. He's a bit neurotic like that; obsessive, you know. Between the two of us, I think he might have a mental health problem. If this cerbero-whatever it is that you are looking for is here, then I guess that it will be on the shelf with other things starting with the letter 'c.'" Sophia knew exactly where the jar was, but she pretended to search for it a little while longer, careful to make sure that Bastian caught sight of her curves from behind. It worked as planned, and Bastian completely forgot why he had come to the coffee shop in the first place.

"Is this the one?" Sophia asked, handing the jar to Bastian, careful to accidentally brush her hand against his.

Bastian almost dropped the jar. "Aha! That's it, the very one I'm looking for."

"Will this help you to solve the murder then?" Sophia asked, knowing full well that if Bastian tested it for fingerprints, he would find Emilio's prints, her prints, and Bastian's prints on it. The only suspect whose prints were not on it was Madeleine's, but that was exactly as Sophia wanted. You see, Madeleine as a forensics student would have been careful to hide her tracks.

Bastian carried the jar of Cerbera odollam out into the coffee shop and enquired as to how Emilio had come to have access to this substance.

"I picked it up on my travels to India," Emilio answered rather matter-of-factly. He had nothing to hide.

"So, you admit it then?" Bastian said.

Emilio was starting to feel quite cheesed off. "Admit what, exactly? I've not done anything wrong. I had permission to bring the seeds back through customs, and the fruit is perfectly edible and nontoxic. It's hardly a crime to keep a cupboard full of coffee beans, is it?"

Bastian ordered the two assisting officers to arrest Emilio. If it had been up to Bastian, then all coffee drinkers would and should be arrested for drug use, but it was not the law, not yet anyway. "But when I asked you if you had a secret stash of poison, you told me quite clearly that you did not."

Emilio already had his arms behind him as the two officers fought over who would get to handcuff him. It was rare that they got to use the cuffs in the peaceful mountain resort, and both were glad of a little excitement in their policing life. "Of course I denied it. You asked me if I had any poisons, which I don't. You never asked me if I had any coffee beans or cocoa beans or baking supplies."

"But what about *this* here? This is *poison*." Bastian waved the jar in front of him.

"Look, I'm not being funny, but even water is poisonous if you drink too much of it." Emilio was annoyed now.

Théo did his best to try and help Emilio. "And so is coffee if you drink too much of it … and wine …. and nicotine. Even daddy longlegs are poisonous but you don't go around arresting them, do you?"

Bastian was not listening. He was only interested in arresting Emilio. He turned to Sophia. "Thank you, miss; you have been most helpful. It's just a shame that I can't say the same for your boss."

Chapter 36

Police Cell, Val D'Isera Police Station, Austria:
5th December 2018

It was after lunch by the time that Bastian pushed Emilio into our police cell, and though I was, of course, upset to think that Emilio too was now a suspect in Audrey's murder, I was pleased to get the chance to talk with him and to see if we could come up with a plan together to prove our innocence.

"Emilio," I said, not entirely sure how he would react to seeing us after all that had happened in the last 24 hours. For all I knew, he might think we had dobbed him in, or he might *believe* that it was us who had murdered

Audrey with a doughnut made in his shop. But he was as easy going as ever.

"Are you OK?" Emilio asked. "Did they feed you?"

An officer entered the cell and unstacked three small trays of something unrecognisable. "They did now," I replied. "*If* you can call this food."

"I don't care what it is; I'm starving," Eloise announced, scoffing the tray of mush before her taste buds had time to try and work out what it was supposed to be.

We knew that the murderer had to be Sophia; all we had to do was to prove it and get Bastian to see sense.

"OK, let's compare notes on everything that has happened during the day, see if we can't come up with some clues that might help," Eloise suggested.

I went back over my day, from the moment I had woken up, arrived at the coffee shop, opened up, and baked my first doughnuts of the day. Had my burnt tongue from the hot coffee dulled my taste buds when I tried the mixture? Had I got the wrong ingredients somehow?

"Why did you decide to bake the red velvet doughnuts?" Emilio asked me. "Was it a spur of the moment thing or something that was planned?"

I thought about it for a moment, remembering the note that Emilio had left for me on the coffee counter, and Sophia's recipe and a sticky note on the kitchen table. I suddenly had a feeling that I had been set up. "Well, normally, I just bake whatever I fancy, but Sophia had suggested that I bake the red velvet doughnuts, and she had given me very precise instructions."

"Go on," Emilio encouraged.

"I was going to bake more of the breakfast doughnuts since you left me that note to say that the chalets had placed extra orders."

Emilio looked at me blankly. "Note? What note?" It suddenly occurred to me that the writing on the two notes was written in the same pen and similar but not the same handwriting, but it was not like Emilio's usual writing. At the time, I had just assumed he had written it in a hurry.

"Oh, heck!" I gasped. "You don't suppose I did bake poisonous doughnuts, do you? Maybe Sophia switched the jars around or poisoned the ingredients?"

Eloise shook her head. "Not possible. I'm afraid that I have a little confession to make myself. I stole one of those doughnuts and ate it in secret. I knew they would go fast, and they just looked so delicious."

I kissed Eloise. Normally, I might have been a

little bit cross with her for stealing my bakes, but if Eloise had eaten the doughnut and not died, then I was in the clear.

Emilio looked glum. "I have to confess to stealing one of the doughnuts as well, and *I'm* still alive. I gave one to Théo when no one was looking, and to Camilla, and Francesca, to cheer them up after the coffee incident with Stefan."

The three of us smiled. "Well, then. I think that proves that my doughnuts were *not* poisoned. And if Sophia did write both of those notes, then that's evidence surely?"

"Only if you still have them," Emilio said.

I smiled. "I do, as it happens. You see, I'm putting together a scrapbook of recipes for when we get back to Mrs Tiggywinkle's, and I tucked the pages in my recipe book. They should still be there."

Eloise was mulling things over. "But if your doughnuts weren't poisoned, then where did the doughnuts come from, and how did Audrey get her hands on them?"

Emilio retraced his steps. "Well, now, I left Sophia baking in the kitchen when I went to talk to Camilla and Francesca. It was when it was busy, but I didn't want to get in the way in the kitchen, so I thought it best to leave you girls, to it. There's only so much room out on the front counter and I'd have got in the way if I'd tried to take orders or made coffees, but Sophia said she wanted to bake something special as a treat for Théo's birthday. It was cooking in the oven when I left, and she wouldn't let me see it in case I ruined it as it cooked. That sounds *awful*, doesn't it? Imagine that, a man who owns a coffee shop but can't bake or make decent coffee to save his life! That's why I leave it to the experts. I'm much better at yoga."

I had a moment of inspiration as things began to fall into place. "That would explain why Sophia went crazy at us when we cleared the tables and brought the dirty dishes in. Now I think about it, I was surprised to see some red food colouring on the chopping board in the dishwasher. I'm always careful to tidy up after myself when I bake, and I know I cleaned away my things before we opened the shop this morning, so why was there red colouring on a chopping board, unless Sophia had made a new batch of doughnuts?"

Emilio had an epiphany too. "And *why* were the doughnuts still warm when I bagged them up and gave them to Stefan as an apology for Sophia's outburst; it was Sophia who suggested I give them to him by way of an apology."

"There's one problem," Eloise pointed out. "If Sophia poisoned the doughnuts and told you to give them to Stefan as an apology, then how come Stefan wasn't poisoned, only Audrey?"

"You don't think that she meant to poison Stefan, do you?" I asked. "Maybe Audrey wasn't the target at all."

"But how do we prove our innocence, especially when we're stuck in here, and Sophia is out there? You don't think she'll poison anyone else, do you?" Emilio asked.

I decided that it was time for Eloise and me to let Emilio in on our secret research work with Théo. I just hoped that he wouldn't be upset with us for not including him earlier.

"There's something we need to tell you. We were worried that Sophia might not have been telling us the truth about her time at culinary school, so we asked Théo to help us find out whether what Audrey said about Sophia not being top of the cohort was true."

"And? What was the result? Was she telling the truth?" Emilio asked, keen to know the answer.

"We don't know yet. Théo was about to find out, but we've not been able to speak to him since we got locked up."

I was suddenly concerned that Emilio's arrest would leave Sophia and Théo alone in the coffee shop together, and I hoped that Théo would not confront her directly if he did know the answer.

There was no accounting for what Sophia might do to him or whether he might be her next victim.

Emilio put his hand on his head. "It's up to Théo to save us? Let's just hope that he's as good at solving murders as he is at doing crosswords. Otherwise, we're doomed."

Chapter 37

Snow Mountain Café, Val D'Isera Ski Resort,
Austria: 5th December 2018

Théo wasn't exactly thrilled at the prospect of being left alone in the coffee shop with Sophia, but Emilio was his friend, and he knew that Emilio was depending on him to look after the coffee shop whilst he was at the police station. The problem was, Théo knew that he was now in danger of being murdered himself after witnessing Sophia turn Emilio in to the police. Part of him wanted to stay at the coffee shop and lock up and make sure that the building was secure, but to do so would mean putting himself at risk from Sophia. He had to act fast, even if it did put the coffee shop in danger of having the cash register robbed in an unstaffed shop.

Thankfully, escape came when he least expected it. He knew exactly who was phoning him and that this was not a conversation he could have right here in front of the very person the call was about, regardless of what the findings were.

Théo hurriedly put on his coat and tried to act as calmly and normally as he could. The caller's number stopped flashing as he missed picking it up in time, but he would call them back in a moment, once he knew he was safe.

He walked as quickly as he could towards the ski shop. It was public enough to be seen in case Sophia followed him and tried to kill him, but private enough that he could have his phone call without it being overheard by anyone of importance. He scurried into the shop and headed toward where Daan was busy sorting out some ski equipment.

"I can't explain right now, Daan, but I need to make a phone call, and I'm worried that Sophia might have followed me. If you see her, promise me you'll do everything you can to distract her? It's a matter of life and death, and I mean that in the literal, not the figurative sense."

"Sure thing, buddy," Daan reassured him a little nervously.

Théo called the culinary school back and spoke to the dean.

"Hi, this is Théo; I'm just returning your call about the culinary competition. I believe I have two of your former students as finalists, and I just need to confirm a few things before we announce the winner. I'd hate to get any of the facts wrong, and I'm a little embarrassed to admit to the two finalists that I've lost their original entry forms. Honestly, I'm such an idiot."

"Certainly," replied the dean. "What exactly do you need to know?"

Théo was surprised that his plan was working so well, especially in this era of data protection and GDPR. "Now I'm not sure which way round it was. Did Sophia Saner get the highest grade in the cohort, or was it Audrey Flandin? I'd hate to embarrass myself by getting it wrong."

"No problem at all. It was Audrey Flandin, quite an exceptional student by all accounts. Dedicated and hard-working. We presented her with a special award at the graduation ceremony. Our highest achiever ever, and youngest to win the accolades she has. She's going to make any restaurant that employs her very famous indeed. Mind you, Sophia Saner's an excellent pastry chef too. I think she was a bit disappointed not to be first, but she was a very close second.

273

Always competing, those two, right from day one."

Théo had got his answer. Sophia had indeed lied about being first, and Audrey had been telling the truth all along, at least in part.

"Pssst," came a noise from Daan. "Sophia's just come into the shop if you still need to avoid her."

Daan pointed to the stockroom out back, and Théo crept in as quickly and quietly as he could. He knew he was in great danger, and whilst the stockroom would be the last place that Sophia would think to search to find him, it was also a terrible spot to hide, given that it had no exits other than the door he had come in.

"Ouch!" A voice screamed, scaring Théo half to death. It was coming from the floor and was closely followed by a "shhh" sound.

Théo looked around the dark room, and vaguely made out the shapes of Margot and Karl. "What are you two doing here?" he asked.

"We're hiding from Sophia," Karl whispered.

"But why?" Théo was thoroughly confused now.

Margot asked the same question of Théo, to which he also answered, "Hiding from Sophia."

Théo started tapping in the numbers on his phone. "I think it's time we called the police."

Margot and Karl looked terrified but reluctantly agreed.

BASTIAN HURRIED EMILIO, Eloise, and Madeleine into the police car and set off in the direction of the ski shop as fast as he could. He was desperate to put the police lights and sirens on, but he was concerned that it might alert the murderer to his arrival. He'd never had the opportunity to use the sirens or lights before, and he was bitterly disappointed.

"What's going on?" I asked, but Bastian ignored me.

He pulled up outside the ski shop and ordered us to get out as quickly and quietly as we could. "I'll explain everything later. Just make sure that Sophia doesn't leave the shop, even if you have to bop her on the nose to stop her."

"Umm, OK," I replied, finding the whole thing a bit unconventional. It wasn't every day that a police officer permitted you to punch someone.

We followed Bastian into the shop, just as two more police officers arrived with the other murder suspects; Stefan, Nicklas, Violetta, and Rose. Bastian locked the door behind us. Sophia was already in the shop, and she seemed to be fixated on the stock room behind the counter where Daan was busy working. She was up to something.

Bastian snuck up behind Sophia and was quick off the mark in grabbing her and putting her in handcuffs. "Sophia Saner, I'm arresting you for the murder of Audrey Flandin."

The two officers walked up to the stock room and shouted as they pushed the door open. "You can come out now! The coast is clear."

Three rather wobbly-looking coffee shop customers came out, not entirely sure whether to believe that they were safe, but as they spotted Sophia in handcuffs next to two police officers, they relaxed and looked hugely relieved.

"What do you mean, you're *arresting* me for the murder of Audrey? That's the most ridiculous thing I've *ever* heard." Sophia wriggled and pulled against Bastian.

"Keep still, Miss Saner," Bastian reprimanded her. "Right then, perhaps Madeleine and Eloise would care to explain things just so that everyone is clear once and for all."

I was still amazed that Bastian had finally acknowledged that Sophia was the murderer. He had taken a lot of persuading, but between the three of us, we had produced enough evidence to make a strong case. I did my best to recount everything in detail. What I hadn't realised was that Théo had uncovered more evidence of his own whilst trapped in the storeroom with Karl and Margot.

"Tell them, Karl," Théo encouraged. "I promise you'll feel better for it."

"Um, OK." Karl was petrified and looking rather guilty. "Well, the thing is…well, it was me that stole Audrey's watch up at the glacier. Well, I maybe didn't steal it exactly, but I saw it on the floor, and I knew that it was covered in diamonds, so I decided to keep it and send it to my cousin Miryam in Sweden. She reckoned she could sell it and share the money. But I felt bad about taking it, especially with Audrey being so upset at losing it. I didn't know it was a gift from her father for passing her exams. I thought she wouldn't miss it. So, I put it in my pocket and went to the restaurant to return it. I wanted to explain to Audrey that I'd taken it and to say I was sorry, but she wasn't there, so I left the watch on the side with some flowers and a card. But I swear I didn't leave any doughnuts."

"And did you see anyone when you were there?" I asked, curious as to how Sophia might fit into all this.

Karl nodded. "Yes. Sophia was just leaving as I arrived, but I didn't think she had seen me. Not until after Audrey died, and then Sophia said that she had seen me and that everyone would know I killed Audrey if I didn't keep quiet. I've been trying to avoid her ever since. But I promise I didn't kill Audrey. Why would I? She was always so nice to me."

It all made sense now, and I knew that Bastian couldn't charge Karl for stealing the watch. "But what about the watch? You said you had it in your pocket when you went to Audrey's? How come it was in your drawer at the bar?"

Karl looked remorseful. "Well, the thing is, I left it with the flowers, and I thought that was the end of it, but then it turned up in my drawer, and that made me scared because I knew that Sophia had planted it there. If she could do that, then she could do anything, and I knew I was in big trouble. I was too scared to even sleep in my bed at night. I'm knackered."

"You're a liar, Karl!" Sophia shouted.

"I think you'll find that the only liar here is you, Sophia!" Margot shouted across the room.

Sophia pulled against Bastian again, but he was having none of it. "And what about you, Margot? You tried to murder your own stepdaughter. You're not exactly an innocent."

"That was an accident!" Margot screamed, visibly upset.

This was certainly news to me, but suddenly everything was beginning to make sense.

Margot calmed herself a moment. "I admit that I didn't take the whole divorce thing very well, and *yes*, I did think that if I killed Audrey, I would inherit her trust fund if I could get her to sign it over to me before she married. And I admit that I *was* hoping to kill her at the glacier. But then I had a change of heart. I regretted it immediately."

"So what happened?" I asked, confused as to how Sophia seemed to know so much about Margot's actions up at the glacier.

Margot huffed. "Sophia is what happened. She was blackmailing me. Said she would tell the police and Felix, and Audrey."

"And why was Rose so cross with you? I saw the two of you together; why were you arguing over papers?" I enquired.

"Ask her." Margot pointed at Rose.

"Me?" Rose shouted. "Don't you go dragging me into this, Margot. I was the one trying to stop you from doing something you might regret."

"You were having an affair with my Felix!" Margot sobbed.

"Yes, I was, I am. We love it each other. You know full well that your relationship with Felix has been over for a long time." Rose was quite flushed.

Eloise was doing a better job than me at keeping up with this new information. "But what I don't understand is what your divorce or Rose's affair has to do with Audrey's death?"

"Oh, it's quite simple," Rose said. "Margot wanted Audrey dead so that she could claim Audrey's trust fund for herself, as long as she managed to trick Audrey into signing everything over to her, whereas I was trying to get Audrey to sign a prenuptial agreement so that her money didn't go to her scammer of a fiancée, Stefan, who also happens to be Sophia's boyfriend of several years! It was Felix who figured it out, and he sent me to try and convince Audrey to sign the papers, but Stefan somehow kept her away from me."

By the look on Bastian's face, this was news to him too, and he had not for a moment considered Stefan to be a suspect in Audrey's murder. "Wait, wait. Let me get this straight, Rose. Are you telling me that Stefan and Sophia were both in on this … together?"

Rose was quite cross that Bastian had missed this. "Yes. That's exactly what I'm saying. He knew that Audrey came top in her cohort and that she was planning to open a restaurant of her own here once they were married. But he knew that if she opened her business, he would lose his, so he and Sophia decided to kill her so that they could then run the Sébastien Paris Pâtisserie together. Why do you think Stefan paid Sophia's tuition and living fees? They knew that together they would be unstoppable. And with Sophia working in the Snow Mountain Café in the meantime, she could slowly destroy Emilio's reputation and steal all his recipes and beans in the process."

Everything seemed clear to me now. And I was glad that justice would be done for Audrey's death. She wasn't always the nicest person, that was for sure, but she didn't deserve to die because of her passion for pastry.

Bastian escorted Sophia out to his police car, followed closely behind by his two officers and Stefan. Bastian was rather pleased with how things had worked out, but even more excited at the fact that he could now drive his police car fast through the town with the sirens and lights blazing. He had already decided to take an extended journey back to the police station, via a few winding mountain roads. It would be a reward for all his incredible effort.

I was still standing there a little bit in awe of the idea that we had just solved our very first detective case, at least in part, and more importantly, we had proven our innocence and saved the reputation of our friends.

EMILIO SUGGESTED that everyone come back with him to celebrate at the coffee shop, but assured us that there would be no more doughnuts, not for today anyway. He had something else to celebrate too.

"Before I forget, I want to make a little toast. To my new yoga academy for skiers and snowboarders, and to my new yoga instructor Violetta, who will be running the classes alongside Nicklas."

IF YOU ENJOYED THIS BOOK...

If you enjoyed this book, I would be infinitely grateful if you would consider leaving me a review. Not only will your review give me a little encouragement as a new writer, but it might just help another reader to find and enjoy my story.

Glossary

GLOSSARY

All-Mountain Skis: Skis that you can use in all weather and snow conditions. The person to go to for ski equipment advice in Val D'Isera is, of course, the Dutch ski shop technician Daan van Bree.

Après-Ski: The time of day (or night) when the skiing is over and you can kick off your skis and enjoy some drinks, music, dance, and of course, tell everyone about your epic day on the slopes. Swedish bartender Karl Rehn is the person to go to in Val D'Isera, especially if you want to try out some cocktails.

Backcountry: This is not the place to ski for most of Val D'Isera's tourists. The backcountry means the slopes that are away from the main piste. Only suitable for skiers like Nicklas Rehn. There's no ski rescue here.

Bail: Eloise bails a lot when she skis; in other words, she takes a tumble in the snow.

Balaclava: Margot was wishing she had one of these full face masks whilst walking in the snow one early morning outside the coffee shop. The wind was icy and made her nose run. A balaclava would have kept her toasty warm.

Base: Ski technician Daan knows all about both types of base that you might find at a ski resort. When the tourists of Val D'Isera say that they will meet each other 'back at base' they mean that they will meet up at Daan's store. But the snowboarders have another meaning - base is the underside of their snowboard.

Bomber: I'm pretty sure that Bastian would be a bit of a bomber if he were on the slopes of Val D'Isera. He seems like just the kind of person who might fly down the ski slopes in a rather uncontrolled fashion, thinking he was a pro.

Brain Bucket: Helmet

Bros: Madeleine would be a bit of a bro. A mountain person who was just happy to have fun on the slopes rather than showing off doing stunts or getting paid like a pro.

Bumps: There are lots of bumps or 'novices' on the slopes at Val D'Isera. The ones who are sensible take lessons with Swedish instructor Nicklas. Novices tend to go home with a lot of bumps on their bodies after a day learning the ropes.

Carving: Ski instructor Nicklas has truly mastered the art of carving - turning cleanly on the slope. He's already got trials to join the Swedish Olympic team.

Chatter: For the pros, chatter is when their skis vibrate and they lose contact with the ground. But you might find a lot of people chattering as they wait for the Val D'Isera ski lift too.

Crust: A frozen layer of snow that covers or is covered by softer snow.

Death Cookies: Everyone on the ski resort hates these large chunks of ice that are created by grooming and snowmaking.

Dump: When you wake up to loads of fresh new snow in the morning.

Edge: Very likely an ideal murder weapon - the sharp metal strip found on the edge of skis and snowboards. Used to bite into the snow as you ski or snowboard.

First Tracks: Maddy's favourite thing about going to the coffee shop early in the morning - leaving a trail in the fresh snow for other people to see.

Freerider: Not only is Nicklas a backcountry lover, but he's a freerider too - preferring to ski off-piste, and through the trees.

Freestyle: Skiing or snowboarding with a focus on performing tricks.

French Fries: Newbies and pros alike might do this - skiing with their skis in parallel. Others prefer to pizza.

Gnar: Something both dangerous and cool, often concerning a ski route.

Grooming: Maintenance of the ski slope by trucks and diggers that flatten out the snow.

Jib: A bit like those skateboards who slide along rails and bannisters, except that you do it with skis or a snowboard.

Kicker: A jump that you build when you want to do tricks.

Liftie: A ski lift operator. The best person to speak to if you want to know any gossip.

Line: The proposed route down the slope.

Lunch Tray (aka 'Launch' Tray): Snowboard.

Magic Carpet: A belt-like ski lift that you stand on.

Park Rat: Someone who never leaves the ski resort to explore further afield.

Planker (Two-Planker): Skier.

Pow (Pow-Pow): Light, fluffy and dry powdery snow.

Ripper: An amazing skier who even skis in his or her dreams.

Schussing: Skiing straight downhill without turning.

Scissoring: Crossing ski tips, with edge-to-edge contact.

Shredder: A seasoned snowboarder who knows what's what.

Sick: Awesome.

Six-pack: A chair lift that can carry six people at a time.

Ski Bum: Someone who skis all day rather than working in a proper job.

Snowplough: Novices use this technique to slow down when they ski.

Stomp: If you just stomped that landing, then you just mastered that trick.

Tracked Out: No one likes to ski on snow that has been skied over repeatedly.

Traverse: To ski or zig-zag across a slope.

White Out: When the visibility is rubbish because of the snow.

Wipe Out: A very ungraceful fall or landing whilst skiing or snowboarding.

Traverse: To ski or zig-zag across a slope.

White Out: When the visibility is rubbish because of the snow.

Wipe Out: A very ungraceful fall or landing whilst skiing or snowboarding.

Recipes

RECIPES

Maddy's Pre-Ski Breakfast Doughnuts (makes 4 doughnuts)

I'm sure this is what Maddy would serve up to her ski buddies before a morning on the piste. Hot and filling, the perfect way to start the day.

Ingredients

- 100g dates
- 100g wholemeal self-raising flour
- 100g self-raising flour (keep a little for dusting)
- 30g ground almonds
- 1 large free-range egg
- tiny pinch of sea salt

- 70ml water
- olive oil
- 320g blueberries
- 1 tablespoon runny honey
- 4 tablespoons Greek yoghurt
- ground cinnamon

Method

1. Chop up the dates and remove the stones. Place the dates in a food processor (or cut them small if you are doing this by hand).

2. Add the flour, ground almonds, egg, a tiny pinch of sea salt, 1 egg, and 70ml of water to the food processor or bowl.

3. Combine the ingredients so that it eventually forms a dough ball (this will be super quick to blitz in the food processor, but will take a while by hand).

4. Sprinkle a bit of flour on a counter and put the dough ball on top, kneading it for about 2 minutes.

5. Roll out the dough to approximately 1.5cm

thick, and cut out some circles with a round 8cm cutter or the rim of a glass (a pint glass will do). Use a smaller 3cm cutter to cut out the doughnut hole in the middle.

6. Put the doughnuts you just cut out, to one side, and roll the left-over dough into a new ball, roll it out, and cut out more doughnuts, repeating the process until you have run out of dough.

7. Pour the water into a large saucepan and wait for the water to boil. At this point, you can place your doughnut into the boiling water for 5 minutes, carefully turning them over after two and a half minutes. Remove the doughnuts from the simmering pan, and drain them well.

8. Add one tablespoon of olive oil to a frying pan and heat over medium heat. Place your doughnuts into the frying pan and turn them regularly for about 10 minutes until they are golden brown on both sides. The crustier they are, the better, but don't let them burn.

9. Next, you want to add the blueberries to the pan, along with the honey. Make sure that you keep the pan moving so that nothing burns and

everything gets covered with the blueberry juice and sticky honey.

10. Once the doughnuts look shiny, pour the yoghurt over them in the frying pan. Remove them to your plates for serving, and sprinkle a little cinnamon over the top to make them look pretty.

Sébastien Paris Pâtisserie Chocolate Brioche Doughnuts

These doughnuts are fancy enough to serve in the best of restaurants, even the Sébastien Paris Pâtisserie.

Ingredients

• 500g strong white bread flour (keep a little for dusting)
• 7g salt
• 50g caster sugar
• 10g instant yeast
• 140ml warm full-fat milk
• 5 medium eggs
• 250g unsalted butter

- 200g continental plain chocolate
- 3 litres sunflower oil
- Caster sugar

Method

1. Put the flour, sugar, salt, and yeast into a food processor (or mixing bowl if you don't have a food processor).

2. Add the milk and eggs to the bowl, mix for about 10 minutes until the mixture is smooth and dough-like.

3. Knead the dough and gradually start to fold in the softened butter.

4. Once all of the butter is incorporated into the dough, and it feels sticky and smooth, knead it for another 8-10 minutes until firmer.

5. Place the dough into a larger bowl so that it has plenty of space to rise. Cover the bowl with cling film and place it into the fridge overnight.

6. Remove the bowl of dough from the fridge, and sprinkle some flour onto a worktop. Put the dough onto the worktop and knock it back.

7. Roll the dough into about 20 balls of equal size and flatten each ball out slightly.

8. Break the continental chocolate bar into little pieces, and insert some chocolate into each dough ball, smoothing the dough over the hole where the chocolate was inserted.

9. Place the dough balls onto a lightly floured tray, with space between each ball, and cover the tray with cling film. Leave them for about an hour to rise again. They should double in size.

10. Pour the oil into a saucepan or deep fat fryer and heat the oil to about 180C. Carefully place each dough ball into the fryer or pan. Make sure to turn the doughnuts in the oil so that they cook on both sides and have an equal colour. You need to fry them for 10-12 minutes even if they have changed colour, otherwise, they won't be cooked through, and the chocolate won't melt.

11. Remove the doughnuts from the frying oil and place them onto some kitchen paper to help drain off some of the fat.

12. Sprinkle the doughnuts with caster sugar on all sides, and they are ready to serve.

Karl's Parampampoli Cocktail (makes 1 litre)

Ingredients

- 200ml espresso coffee
- 200ml grappa
- 200ml brandy
- 200ml red wine
- 120g sugar
- 2 tablespoons of wildflower honey

Method

1. Pour all the ingredients into a saucepan, on high heat, and bring to the boil.

2. Remove the pan from the heat and let it cool. Pour the cooled liquid into bottles and shake them every few days. Keep them in a cool, dark place.

3. When you are ready to drink the Parampampoli, pour the liquor into a saucepan, heat it to boiling point, pour into small ceramic cups.

4. Bring a match over the surface of each cup, being **VERY CAREFUL** of your hands because the liquor contains a lot of alcohol and will ignite suddenly with a long-lasting flame.

5. Wait for the flame to go out, or extinguish it yourself, and enjoy.

Have you Read...

Baa'd to the Bone

A sheepdog in training. A flock under threat. Can Beau find a killer before the case unravels?

Beau dreams of being a champion sheepdog just like his aunt. With the help of new livestock friends and a kind-hearted farmer, he vows to lead the herd proudly through the lush valleys of Wales. But when one of the sheep goes missing, Beau never expected a woolly crime scene …

While his aunt warns him not to get too friendly with the flock, Beau's connection with the sheep gets him both respect and a target on his back. As the brave pup frantically sniffs for clues, he's got one chance to solve the mystery before the farm starts counting sheep for all the wrong reasons.

Will Beau learn the ropes in time to protect his friends from a flock fatality?

About the Author

Sarah Jane Weldon is a British cozy mystery author. On an average day, you'll find her working on the set of a new film or television production, ice swimming in a far off place, or plotting an evil character's demise.

Sarah isn't a fan of her middle name 'Jane' (she prefers to be called Sarah) but readers were getting her mixed up with another Sarah Weldon who wrote hot and steamy romance, so she added her middle name 'Jane' to help readers find her.

Outside of writing, Sarah is a crazy cat lady, she has three — Ozzy, Artemis, and Esa — and until Valentine's Day 2019 she had a 15 year old Italian Greyhound called Isla who sadly passed away from cancer. Sarah's publishing company Islà Britannica Books is named after her beloved dog, and she plans to welcome one of Isla's descendants to the family as soon as possible.

Sarah is a fierce advocate for children's equality and literacy and regularly works with schools through Skype in the Classroom, School Speakers, as a STEM Ambassador, and through the UK registered environmental and STEM education charity 'Oceans Project' which she founded with a small group of refugee children whilst working for the Ministry of Education and Science in the former Soviet Republic of Georgia. In 2014 Microsoft Education named Sarah as a 'woman changing the world through technology' for International Women's Day for her work with schools worldwide.

A large percentage of royalties from Sarah's books and paid employment directly supports Oceans Project's work with disadvantaged young people, sending them on Earthwatch expeditions worldwide where they get hands on experience working with sharks, coral reefs, and in the rainforest carrying out citizen science projects with leading experts in the field.

UK readers can support Oceans Project by

shopping on Amazon Smile (www.smile.amazon. co.uk/ch/1156583-0).

Sarah's love for the water was filmed for a Channel 4 documentary series called 'My Family Secrets Revealed' looking at her DNA and family history. You can watch the series on her YouTube channel or on Channel 4 if you are in the UK.

Sarah is the founder of #cozymysteryday, which takes place annually on the 15th September (Agatha Christie's birthday). The day is a chance for readers and authors alike to share their favourite cozy mystery books, movies, and television series with the world.

Where to Find Me

facebook.com/sarahweldonauthor

twitter.com/sarahrowssolo

instagram.com/sarahrowssolo

amazon.com/Sarah-Jane-Weldon

bookbub.com/authors/sarah-jane-weldon

goodreads.com/sarah-weldon

pinterest.com/sarahweldon

youtube.com/sarahrowssolo

The idea for this story was based on my love of coffee, English tea shops, and doughnuts, especially when mixed with time spent in nature doing things like ice swimming.

A huge thank you to everyone who has made this book possible, for beta reading, editing, cover design, and words of encouragement to never give up. Very special thanks to my lovely patrons and Kickstarter backers, without whom I wouldn't be writing at all.

Look Out for Maddy and Eloise's next thrilling
adventure in ...

Extra Shots

Extra Sheets

Lightning Source UK Ltd.
Milton Keynes UK
UKHW040743310520
364200UK00001B/2/J